EVIL FAMILY

WAYNE LAWSON

First published in the United Kingdom in 2025 by
The Cloister House Press

ISBN 978-1-913460-87-7

Chapter 1

Michael Chivers, the younger brother of Jasmine Chivers, was on a mission of opulent significance.

He had broad shoulders, shiny dark hair, his face was lightly sprinkled with acne, and his eyes were hazel. Michael had other features too, he looked solid and decisive.

Michael sat on a comfy chair in a cafe bar he reflected on the radiant town. The town was as beautiful as the garden of Eden. It was shielded by picturesque high ground, watered by lovely streams, carpeted with lovely countless flowers, and shaded by noble trees joyful with the notes of droves of singing birds. Beautiful land stretch of grassland gave the town a captivating outlook. To breathe in the balmy atmosphere was to be conscious of some rarer and finer life, and the beauty of the sunny clear skies marvelous at dawn and with tints of saffron and opal, was like a dream of sweet heaven. A clean, wide sky bent over that town, and the air that moved on it was cool and sweet.

As Michael Chivers stumbled out of the cafe his face was a sickish red and each breath, he drew was an incredible pain. A hard blow in the guts and on the side of the head can do that to a man, and Michael had gotten a hard one. Not with a fist, which would have been wretched enough, but from the end of a socks stuff with two pool balls.

Somehow, he got to the car park and managed to slide onto a seat. But that was all Michael could do. He grumbled as the change in posture cramped his stomach muscles.

Several people walked past as he emits sick into the car park, they were scowling sympathetically, or turning their eyes in revulsion. But Michael was in too much pain to notice or to care if he had. When finally, his tummy felt better, though still not well enough to go anywhere. By then, however, a family car had pulled up behind him, a people cariers car.

'Are you ok, mister?'
'What?'
'You seem very unwell, Mr. Any idea what caused it?'
'My feast, I surmise. I take the point, I should know better, but I had a tuna-mayo salad
and it didn't taste quite right when I was eating it, though. . .' Michael Chivers let his voice trail away, smiling a timid, sorrowful smile.
'Uh-huh!' The man from the family car bobbed firmly. 'Look, you're all right, now? Want us to help you with anything?'
'Oh, no. I'm okay.'
'My daughter is a trained nurse. No trouble to give you the once over.'
Michael declined, cool but fiercely. Any more extended contact with this family would result in his secret reveal. So far only his sister knew he was a sly fox, and he meant to keep it that way.

The man went back to the family car, and he and his daughter drove off. Michael waved a smiling farewell to them and got back onto his feet. Cautiously, flinching a little, he got a cigarette lit. Then, convinced that the last of the sick was over, he forced himself to stand tall.

And suddenly, slowly moving he was back inside the cafe again. Sipping a plastic cup of water at the fountain, while he casually studied his surroundings.

It was a nice clean establishment with an abbreviated water fountain, a showcase or two of nuts, crisps, and candy, and overflowing racks of paperback books, and greeting cards. In the South, such cafe's were referred to as bistros or brasserie. Here they were usually called tea rooms or cafeterias.

Chivers and two elderly ladies were the only customers in the cafe. The one other person present was the cafe owner, a large, chubby looking bald head man of perhaps fourty or fourty two. As Chivers finished his drink, he observed the bald head man's manner as he drew liquid down from the fridges, working with a confusing mixture of attentiveness and indifference. He knew exactly what needed to be done, his expression said, and to hell with doing a little more than that. Nothing for show, nothing to sway anyone. The boss, Chivers decided, putting down his plastic cup and sliding off the chair. He strolled up toward the counter, and the bald head man laid down the sock stuff with two pool balls with which he had been pounding. Then, wiping his hands on his apron, he also moved up to the register.

'Ten bucks,' he said.

'And a package of those roasted peanuts, too.'

'Fifteen bucks.'

'Fifteen bucks hmm?' Michael began to muddle around his pockets, while the bald head man fidgeted impatiently. 'Now, I know I've got some change here. Must have. I wonder where the hell. . .'

Annoyed, he shook his head and drew out his wallet. 'I'm sorry. Mind cashing a fifty?'

The man almost snatched the bill from his hand. He whacked the bill down on the cash register ledge and counted out the change from the drawer. Michael Chivers absently picked it up, continuing his muddle around search of his pockets.

'Now, doesn't that get you? I mean, you know darned well you've got something, but--' He broke off, eyes widening with a pleased smile. 'There it is--fifteen bucks! Just give me back my fifty, will you?'

The cashier grabbed the fifteen bucks from him, and tossed back the fifty bucks. Michael turned casually toward the door, pausing, on the way out, for an unconcerned glance at the paper supplement display.

Hence, for the fourth time that day, he had worked the fifties, one of the several natural ploys of the short swindle grift. The other being a slap, usually good for bigger scores but not nearly so swift nor safe. Some marks fall for the fifties repeatedly, without ever tipping.

Michael didn't see the bald headed man come around the counter. The man was just there, all of a sudden, a sulky snarl on his face, swinging the socks stuff with two pool balls like a baseball player.

'Grubby thief,' he roared angrily. 'Grubby thief keeps cheating me and robbing me, and my misses swear me out for it!'

The base of the sock landed in Michael's chest. Even the cashier was surprised by its effect. 'Now, you can't blame me, you mugger,' he stuttered. 'You were asking for it. I--I give you change for fifty bucks, and then you have me give the fifty back, an'-- an' '--his self-righteousness begins to fall apart. 'Now, you know you did, wrong you poacher.'

Michael could think of nothing but his agony. He turned swimming eyes on the cashier, eyes flooded with pain filled baffled. The look completely demolished the cashier.

'It was just a mistake, mister. You made a mistake, and I made a mistake!' He backed away, terrified. 'Don't look at me like that!'

'You destroyed me,' Michael wheezed. 'You shattered me, you rotten bastard!'

'Nah! Please don't say that, man!'

'I'm dying,' Michael wheezed. And, then, somehow, he had gotten out of the cafe.

And now, seated in a taxi and re-examining the incident, he could see no reason to fault himself, no blemish in his technique. It was just bad luck. He'd simply caught a dunce, and clowns couldn't be figured out.

Michael was right about that. And he'd been right about something else, although he didn't know it.

As the taxi drove Michael back to home, constantly braking and speeding up in the thickening traffic, repeatedly stopping and starting, with every passing second and every minute, he was feeling ill.

Chapter 2

Michael Chivers's older sister Jasmine Civers was not a loyal family member. She's five years older than Michael. A few months after her eighteenth birthday, their parents suffered an accident which made them orphan. Thanks to the circumstances of its happening, it also made her well-off by the town standards. A whole acre of property and thousands of dollars a month to spend on herself. Which was right where she meant to spend it.

Settling down in Castries, she found lucrative and unselective employment as a pole dancer. Or, more accurately, it was unselective as far as she was concerned. Jasmine Chivers wasn't putting out for anyone; not, at least, for a few bucks or drinks. Her nominal heartlessness often aggrieved the customers, but it drew the favorable attention of her employers. After all, the world was full of skirts, drifters who could be had for a grin or a gin. But a smart kid, a doll who not only had looks and class, but was also smart, well, that kind you could use.

They used her, in increasingly responsible magnitudes. As a managing hostess, as a recruiter for a chain of establishments, as a minder of sticky-fingered and bungling employees; as courier, liaison officer, finger woman; as a collector and outlay. The money poured in, but little of the shower settled on her younger brother Michael.

Jasmine wanted to pack him off to college, only drawing back, furious, when the figures were quoted to her. A few thousand dollars annually, plus a lot of extras, and just for taking care of a younger brother! Just for keeping a brother out of trouble! Why, for that much money she could buy several nice fur clothing.

They must think she was a dupe, she decided. Pain in the neck that he was, she'd just look after Michael herself. And he'd darned well keep out of trouble or shed skin him alive.

She was, of course, infused with certain immortal instincts,crumbled and withered though they were; so she had her occasional moments of conscience. Also, certain things had to be done, for the sake of appearances: to suffocate charges of neglect and the unpleasantness agreeable to that. In either case, obviously, and as Michael instinctively knew, whatever she did was for herself, out of fear or as a comfort for her conscience.

Generally, her attitude was that of a selfish older sister to an annoying little brother. They rowed with each other. She delighted in swallowing down his share of some treat, while he motioned about her in helpless rage.

'You're mean! Just a dirty old monster, that's all!'

'Don't you call me names, you arrogant brute!', striking at Michael. 'I'll teach you!'

'Teach me, Teach me! Don't even have enough sense to say 'teach!'

'I do, too! I did say 'teach!'

Michael was an excellent student in school, and exceptionally well-behaved. Learning came easily for him, and good behavior seemed clearly a matter of common sense. Why risk irritation when it doesn't make you anything? Why be profitlessly detained after the center of learning when you could be out hustling fruits, or vegetables, or running errands? Time was money, and money was what made the world go around.

As one of the smartest and best-behaved boys in his classes, he naturally drew the displeasure of the other kind. But no matter how cruelly or frequently he was attacked, Jasmine offered only mocking condolence.

'Only one arm?' she would say, if he exhibited a bruised or swollen arm.

Oddly enough, Michael found a certain comfort in her backhanded comments. On the surface they were worse than nothing, merely insults added to wound, but beneath them lay a chilling and callous science of thought. A grim performance on the other hand stands damned philosophy which could accommodate itself to anything but blankness.

He had no liking for Jasmine, but he came to commend her. She'd never given him anything but a hard time, which was about the extent of her kindness to anyone. But she'd done all right. She knew how to take care of herself.

She showed no soft spots until he was entering his teens, a handsome, wholesome-looking youth with dark hair and wide-set hazel eyes. Then, to his furtive delight, he began to note a refined change in her attitude, a softening of her voice when she spoke to him and a quelled hunger in her eyes when she looked at him. And seeing her thus, knowing what was behind the change, he was overjoyed in teasing her.

Was something wrong? Did she want him to move out of the home for a while and leave her alone?

'Oh, no, Michael. Really. I like being together with you.

'Now, Jasmine. You're just being polite. I'll get out of your way right now.'

'Please, my little brother . . .' Biting her lip at the usual endearment, a humble flush spreading over her lovely features. 'Please stay with me. After all, I'm your older sister.'

'I'll leave right now, Jasmine. I know you want me to. You just don't want to hurt my feelings.'

She laughed shakily, and called him ditzy; avoiding his eyes, refusing to be spurned as she must have known she would be.

'Of course, I want you to stay, we have money! I've got plenty, and anything I have is yours. You--'

"Anything I have is yours,' 'Michael, eyes narrowed noticeably. 'That would make a good title for a song, Jasmine.'

'You can go to one of the really good colleges, Michael. Monroe or Destiny college, or some place like that. Your grades are certainly good enough, and with my money--our money . . .'

'Now, Jasmine. You know you need the money for yourself. You always have.'

She winced, as though he had struck her, and her face worked puny, and the trim size-eight suit seemed suddenly to hang on her: an evil moral to a life that had gotten her everything and given her nothing. And for a moment, he almost changed his mind. He almost sympathizes with her.

And then she spoiled it all. She began to cry, to sob like a young child, which was a brainless, crazy thing for Jasmine Chivers to do; and to top off the ridiculous and embarrassing performance, she threw on the corn.

'Don't be mean to me, Michael. Please, please don't. You're breaking my heart . . .'

Michael laughed out loud. He couldn't restrain himself.

'Only one heart, Jasmine?' he said.

Chapter 3

Michael Chivers moved into a holiday let apartment called the Park Royal, a name which hinted at a grandeur that was wholly non-existent. It boasted ten rooms, all unsuited, but it was purely a boast.

It was a two-story affair with a grey stone facade, and a small, red carpet floored lobby. The receptionist was an elderly pensioner, who was delighted to work for a very small salary and a free room. With such arrangements as these, the service left something to be desired. But, as the quickly jovial proprietor pointed out, anyone who was moving hastily could hurry right on out to one of the countries most finest hotels or guest houses, where he could doubtless get a nice little room for a hundred bucks a day instead of the Park Royal's minimum of nine hundred a month.

Broadly speaking, the Park Royal was little different than the numerous other guest houses and hotels which are strung out along St Jude Highway and other arterial streets of Castries; establishments catering to families, couples, and working men and women who required a close-in address. Mostly, these latter, single people, were contractors, white collar workers for the landlord was strongly prejudiced against unattached women.

'Oh, I tell you, Mr. Chivers. I've hotelled all over this wonderful world of ours, and I'm telling you that hookers and hotellin' just don't mix. It's against the divine being laws, and it's against man's laws. You'd think the law enforcement officers would be too busy catching real criminals, instead of snooping around for courtesans, but that's the way the gravy stains, as the saying is, and I don't fight it. An ounce of avoidance, that's my proverb. If you keep out the chicks, you keep out the bawds, and you've got a nice clean respectable place like this hotel, without a lot of law enforcement officers hanging around. Why, if a police comes in here now, I know he's a new man, and I tell him he'd better come back after he checks with headquarters. And he never comes back, Mr. Chivers; he's damned well told that it ain't necessary, because this is a hotel not a massage parlour.'

'I'm pleased to hear that, Mr. Harper,' Michael said truthfully. 'I've always been very careful where I lived.'

'Right. A man's got to be,' Harper said. 'Now, let's see. You wanted a king size room suite, say, a sitting room, bedroom, and bath.'

He inquired about the rental of the suite. Harper approached the issue prolixly, pointing out the necessities of maintaining a first-rate clientele, for he would settle for nothing less, by the divine, and also making a profit, which was goddamn hard for an honest man to do in these times.

'Why, some of these farmhands we get in here, I mean that attempt to get in here, they'll fight you for a wear-out light orb. You just can't please them, know what I mean? It's like being skillful, you know, the more they get the more they want. But that's the way the cookie crumbles, I guess, and like we used to say down in Castries, if you can't live in a glass house you better not throw stones.For you, seven hundred and twenty five a month, Mr. Chivers?'

'That sounds reasonable,' Michael smiled. 'I'll take it.'

'I'm sorry, Mr. Chivers. I'd like to shade it down a little for you; I ain't saying I wouldn't shade it for the right kind of tenant. If you'd guarantee, now to stay a minimum of four months, why--'

'Mr. Harper,' said Michael.

'Why, I could make you a special rate. I'll lean over backward to--'

'Mr. Harper,' Chivers said firmly. 'I'll take the place on a six month lease. First and last month's rent in advance. And seven hundred and twenty-five a month will be fine.'

'It will?' The landlord was incredulous. 'You'll lease for six months at seven hundred and twenty-five.'

'I will. I make a profit in my business, and I expect others to make one in theirs.'

Harper murmured. He puffed. His beer belly wriggled in his pants, and his entire face, including the area which extended back into his receding head, reddened with pleasure. He was a shrewd and practiced student of human nature, he proclaimed. He knew farmhands when he saw them, and he knew gentlemen; he'd immediately spotted Michael Chivers as one of the latter.

'And you're intelligent,' he nodded wisely. 'You know it just ain't good business to swindle where you live. What the hell? What's the percentage in swindling a hotel for a few bucks, people you're going to see every day, if it's going to make them a little down on you?'

'You're definitely right,' Chivers said warmly.

The Park Royal was the seventh hotel he'd visited since his arrival from the lower end of Castries. All had offered quarters which were equal to and as inexpensive or low-end than those he had taken here.

For there is a chronic glut of rooms in Castries smaller guest houses. But he had found obscurely indefinable objections to all of them. They didn't look quite up to his standards. They didn't feel quite right. Only the Park Royal and Mr Harper had the right feel and look.

'One more thing,' Harper was saying now. 'This is your home, see? leasing like you do, it's just the same as if you were in an apartment or house. It's your castle, like the law says, and if you want to have a guest, you know, a lady guest, why you got a perfect right to.'

'Thank you for telling me,' Michael nodded seriously. 'I don't have anyone in mind at the moment, but I usually make lady friends wherever I go.'

'Of course. A tall handsome looking young fellow like you is bound to have lady friends, and I bet they got class too. None of these roundheels that crumb a place up just by walking through the hallway.'

'Never,' Michael Chivers assured him. 'I'm very careful of the friends I make, Mr. Harper. Particularly the lady friends.'

He was careful. During his three year tenancy at the Park Royal he had had only one female visitor, an upper class girl in her mid twenties, and everything about her looks, dress, and attitude was ample satisfactory even to the discriminating Mr. Harper. The only fault he could find with her was that she did not come often enough. Cause Emily Casey was also discriminating. Given her own way, something that Michael frequently refrained from giving her as a matter of policy, she wouldn't have come within a mile of the Park Royal. After all, she had a very nice apartment of her own, a place with one bedroom, a sitting room, two baths and a large posh kitchen.

'Flattery will get you nowhere, young lad' Emily was pleased. 'I'm four years older, and she feels every minute of it.'

Michael grinned. Four years older?

'Well ... I guess I could come over and spend some time with you'

'That's my girl. I'd hold my breath if I wasn't breathing so heavily.'

'Mmm? Let's hear you.'

'Huff, puff,' Michael said.

'You poor thing,' Emily said. 'Emily hurried just as fast as she could.'

It appears that she had been dressed to go out when Michael called, for she arrived in less than half an hour. Or, perhaps, it only seemed that way. He had got up to unlock the door initially to her arrival, and returning to bed he had felt strangely tired and faint. So he had let his eyes move slowly close, and when he opened them, a very little later seemingly, she was entering the room. Gliding into it on her tiny, spike-heeled shoes; with glossily black hair, and direct angel eyes.

She paused just inside the doorway for a moment, self-assured but entreating. Posing like one of those super models on a catwalk. Then, she reached behind her, feeling for and finding the door key. And turning it with a soft click.

His silent approval spoke to her, and she gave a little twitch to her body, letting the coat steal hang from one shoulder. Then, hips swaying delicately, she came slowly across the room; small chin outthrust; seemingly tugged forward by her nicely shaped body within the small blue blouse.

She stopped with her knees pressed against his bed, and looking upward he could see nothing but the tip of her nose above the contours of her breasts.

Emily's glance was electric, and it was impossible to see her look unmoved, she exhaled an atmosphere of delightfulness of the most maddening force. Her singular beauty, and the nameless charm that infused her, seemed to have an irresistible attraction for him. Every time that Michael's eye rested on her she trembled intensely, and seemed drudging under some mysterious and powerful influence. Her lovely breasts heaved, and the humidity of her eyes increased.

Michael was still keeping his eyes fixed on beautiful young Emily. He appeared intensely excited, his nostrils were dilated, he breathed hard, and his eyes seemed to burn in their sockets.

The young Emily. Had an exquisitely shaped head graced a neck and shoulders, full liquid eyes, and long lashes, a nose of perfect form, and two ruby glowing lips that seemed made to be kissed slowly and hard.

Her form was magnificent, of medium height, widely spreading hips, and a bosom of small proportions, the firmness of which rendered stays entirely unnecessary; a fact that was evident on watching the rise and fall of her two lovely breasts, their form being perfectly defined even to the nipples, beneath her well-fitting clothing.

They sat down, and Michael's arm wound round the young woman's enticing waist, and he could not resist kissing those lovely soft looking lips. She trembled like an aspen, as he gazed into her moist and humid eyes.

'You beautifier, do you know what you are implying?'

'Yes Mr Handsome,' she replied.

'Do you fancy me?'

'Passionately,' was her reply.

'What would you like to do to prove that passion?'

'Anything you desire.'

'Okay, I wish for you to slowly undress.'

She consented at once. This attractive young woman standing before him; lovely ankles, calves, and bare feet and those enchanting breasts peeking over her bra, constituted a most curvy sight. He then desired her to rise and kneel on the love seat, then coming behind her Michael gently pulled apart the cheeks of her divine honey pot, and disclosed the little slit that lay nestling between them. Her enticing thighs with a very pretty little opening. Altogether it was a very desirable inspection, and Michael thought that failing anything better he might manage to find a good deal of enjoyment in her charms. He burned to fuck her, but dared not rove just yet, Slipping off his underwear, therefore, he jumped up beside her on the love seat, and threw his arms around her.

Michael was more pleased than offended at her proceedings, which she seasoned with repeated kisses and exclamations, such as 'What a charming creature thou art! ' she gave him a kiss that seemed to exhale her soul through her lips. What pleasure she had found Michael comprehended quite quickly, but this he knew, that the first sparks of kindling nature, the first ideas of pollution, were caught by him that evening; and that the acquaintance and communication with the bad of their sex, is often as exciting to innocence as all the seductions of the other.

Her gallant began first, as she arose, to disengage, her breasts, and restore them to the liberty of nature, with no more than a pair of jumps; but on their coming out to brighter view, they both thought a new light was added to the room, so flawlessly shining was her devine body; then they rose in so happy a swell as to compose her a well horned fullness of bosom, that had such an effect on the eye as to seem flash hardened into a luminous body, of which it mirrored the polished gloss, and far surpassed even the most beauty, in the life and radiance of a heavenly view. Which man could refrain from such provoking enticements in reach? Michael touched her breasts, first lightly, when the glossy smoothness of the skin slipped away from his hand, and made it slip along the surface; he pressed them, and the resilient flesh that filled them, thus pitted by force, rose again springing back with his hand.

At times Michael took his hands from the semi-breasts of her bosom, and transferred the pressure of them to those medium ones, which he squeezed, clutched and played with, until at length in pursuit of driving, so hotly urged, brought on the height of the position, with such overpowering pleasure, that his fair partner became now necessary to support him, panting, almost keel over, and dying as he entered her honeypot; He willed her to take his manhood and insert it in that divine vent again, and to his intense joy he succeeded in burying himself in her very hard, with which she no sooner felt the grueling sweetness of, than unable to keep her legs, and yielding to the mighty intoxication, she swerved, and falling forward on the bed, made it a necessity for him, if he would preserve the warm-pleasure hold, to fall upon her, where they honed, in a continued conjunction of body and ecstatic flow, their scheme of joys for that time.   Michael placed his fingers within her slit and rubbed them about in the moisture, and then substituted his middle finger, rubbing luxuriously the lips and clitoris, and thrusting in the velvet tip as far as it would go into the honey pot, until Emily speak in undertone, 'It is coming again, Michael Oh! Oh! Rub and fuck harder, my dear.'

Michael stared at her, and turning towards her, kindly enquired how she felt? and, scarce giving her time to answer, embossed on her lips one of his burning rapture kisses, which raced a flame to her heart, that from thence radiated to every part of her; and presently, as if he had proudly meant satisfaction for the exploration she had smuggled of all his naked beauties.   Michael wrapped her legs up as high as it would go, took his turn to feast his eyes on all the gifts nature had bestowed on her body; his busy hands, too, reached intemperately over every part of the young Emily. The delicious stiffness and hardness of her yet unripe swelling breasts, the glossy and firmness of her flesh, the freshness and regularity of her features, the harmony of her limbs, all seemed to confirm him in Michael's satisfaction with his bargain; but when curious to examine the devastation he had made in the center of his over fierce attack, he not only directed his hands there, but with a couple of cushions put under, placed her pleasingly for his lustful purpose of exploration. Then, who can exibit the ignition his eyes glistened, his hands glowed with!

whilst sighs of pleasure, and tender broken yells, were all the praises Michael could voiced. By this time his manhood, stiffly risen at her, gave Emily to see it in its highest condition and bravery. Michael looked at it himself, he felt very pleased at its condition, and, smiling loves and graces, seized her waist, and carried it, with relentless compulsion, to this pride of nature, and its richest triumph and marvelous feat. They twist and turn like two serpents, their bodies arched, and then they fall prone on each other, every muscle vibrating as they cum in all the agonies of lasciviousness.

Michael. However, is much more than a ruthless stallion, he had stamina in abundance. He was then lying at length upon that bed, the scene of Emily's polite joys, as she came back from the bathroom, which was with all the art of negligence flowing loose, and in a most tempting order: no clothing whatsoever. On the other hand, Emily stood at a short distance, that gave her a full view of a fine featured, shapely, healthy young lad, breathing the sweets of fresh blooming youth; Michael's hair, which was of a perfect shining black, played to his face in natural side curls, and was set out with a smart skin fade at the back; his powerful legs, shewed the shape of a muscular well made thigh; altogether composed a figure of pure power.

Emily offered Michael to come towards her, smiling in Michael's face, took his hands, and immediately drew him towards her, pretending to be blushing; for surely Michael's extreme shyness, called for, at least, all the advances to encourage him: Michael was so restless and excited and could not wait any longer; his big manhood was still stiff, and every nerve throbbed. His body was now conveniently leaned towards her, and just softly tossing his lightly stubbled chin, she then took, and carrying his hands to her breasts, she pressed it tenderly to them. Her breasts were now finely furnished, and raised in flesh, so that, gasping with desire, they rose and fell, in short heaves, under his touch: at this, Michael's eyes began to gleam with all the fires of inflamed nature, and the sides of his face flushed with a deep crimson: loss of words with joy, rapture, Michael could not speak, but then his looks, his emotion, this fired him anew, and placing both hands beneath her buttocks, he pressed her honey pot towards him with the utmost force, while driving in and out of her with deep and body-killing thrusts. Sufficiently satisfied her, and that she had no regrets to qualm.

Her lips, which she threw in Michael's way, so that he could not escape kissing them, fixed, fired, and emboldened him: and now, glancing her eyes towards that part of his body which covered the essential object of enjoyment, she clearly recognized the swell and commotion there; she was indeed no longer able to contain herself, she could both see and feel a rigid hard physique. Curious then, and yearning to unfold so alarming a mystery, as it were, which were bursting ripe from the active force within, those of his waistband and frontal harder at a touch, when she saw, with wonder and surprise, what? not the toy of a boy, but a hard pole, of so broad a standard, that had proportions been observed, it must have belonged to a young gargantuan. Yet the young Emily could not, without pleasure, behold, and even set forth to experience, such a size such a breadth of animated stature! perfectly well turned and fashioned, the elevated stiffness of it. In summary, it stood as both an object of dread and joyfulness.

Dear me the fiery touch of his fingers dictated her, and her fears melting away before the glowing intolerable heat, her thighs disclosed themselves, that honey pot, and surrendered all freedom to his hand: and now, a fitting movement that made the avenue lay so fair, too open to be missed.

By her direction, however, the head of his prick was so captiously pointed, that, feeling Michael onward against the soft opening, a pleasing motion from her met his timely thrust, by which the lips of it, energetically dilated, gave way to Michael thus aided impulsiveness, so that they might both feel that he had gained a fixedness. Hounding then his point, Michael soon, by violent, and, to her, most painful piercing thrusts, wedges himself at length so far in, and she now felt such a mixture of pleasure and pain, as there is no giving a definition of. The sense of pain, however, victorious from his colossal size and stiffness, acting upon her in those continued hard thrusts, with which he furiously followed his penetration, made her cry out gently: 'Oh, my Romeo, I'm in pain!' This was enough for Michael to show her is respectful boyish side; and he immediately drew out the cause of her complaint, whilst his eyes fluently expressed, at once, his sorrow for giving her so much pain, and his hesitance at dislodging from her honey pot, of which the warmth and closeness had given him a gust of pleasure, that he was now desire mad to satisfy, and yet so young not to be afraid of her withholding his comfort, on account of the pain he had put her through.

However, Emily, wasn't pleased with Michael having too much consideration for her poignant blurts; for now, more fired with the manhood before her as it still stood with the fiercest boner, and displayed its broad size, she gave Michael a gentle kiss, which he repaid her with a zeal that seemed at once to express his gratitude to her, and soon replaced herself in a posture to receive, at all peril, the renewed invasion, which Michael did not lag an instant.

Michael commenced to frig her, at first gently, gradually increasing the rapidity and depth of his insertion, till, with a shriek of rapture painful, however, as she was, with his thrusts, which he was so nevertheless as to manage by all angles and degrees, she dared not to complain. In the meanwhile, he made sure, by his huge pole, thick, indriven engine, sensible, at once, to the lovely pleasure of the feel and the pain of the swelling, let him in about three-fourths of the way, when all the most excitable activity he now exerted, to further his penetration, gained him the strength of his purpose: kept up by the pain she had coped with in the course of the session, from the insufferable size of his pole, which was not only long but wider than a cucumber, though it was not as yet in above three-fourths its length.

The well inspired Michael, hot stallion was now satisfactorily in for making her know he was the driver. He had made a little pause, then he still kept his post, he proceeded and open to himself an entire entry into her honey pot, the active power of his thrusts, now gave a brutal lunge, and excited to madness by the shrieks of agony and helpless struggles of the poor young Emily, was buried in her in a moment, Michael's ruthless machine breaking or tearing through every obstacle, favored by the deeply felt impulse of her motions, the soft oiled zones can no longer stand so effective a prise open, but accepting defeat the zone open him deeper entrance. And now, Michael sticks, penetrates, and at length, winning his way slowly but surely, gets entirely in, and finally, a crafted thrust sends it up to the shield. Michael's youthful eyes sparkled with more joyous fires, and all his looks and motions saluted the excess of pleasure, which she now began to share, for she was very sick with delight! stirred beyond bearing with its furious turbulences within her, and glutted and crammed, even to a surfeit. There she was gasping, panting, his eyes twinkling with humid fires, thrusting more furious, and an increased stiffness of his manhood. Hence they continued for some moments, they proceeded with more immense thrust to carry this into effect, lashing her bottom, loins, inside her thighs, and even the lips of her honey pot, tightly distended around the huge manhood of Michael, till the hue of her skin was a burning crimson. Lost, breathless, senseless of everything, and in every part but those adored ones of nature, in which all that they both enjoyed of life and sensation was now totally distilled.

Originality ever makes the sturdy feelings, and in pleasures, especially; no wonder then, that Michael was swallowed up in raptures of admiration of things so interesting by their nature, and now seen and handled so expertly. On the young Emily's part, she was amply overpaid for the pleasure, naked and free to his loosest wish, over the artless, natural stripling: Michael eyes streaming fire, his cheeks glowing with a florid red, his passionate frequent sighs, whilst his hands convulsively squeezed, opened, pressed together again; and all demonstrated the excess, the riot of joys, in having his lewdness thus temperament, that bid him sweet defiance in wordless display, squeezes in, and, driving with refreshed rage, and plugs up the whole passage of that soft venus, where Michael makes all vibrate again.

Emily was now so bruised, so pounded, with Michael's overmatch, that she could hardly stir, or raise herself, but lay quivering, till the fever of her senses let up by degrees, and the hour striking at which she was compelled to stop Michael from anymore frenzy. Emily tenderly gave hints to him of the necessity there was for slowing down; at which she felt as much indignation as he could do, who seemed eagerly inclined to keep the field, and to enter on a fresh action. But the riskiness was too great, and after some hearty kisses of leave, and recommendations of secrecy and discretion.

Michael now kissed her furiously, thrusting his tongue into Emily's mouth, causing her to feel the most extraordinary sensations.

'You're so tasty, girl,' he said, 'what did you think of my frigging skills, have I not got a big manhood and you an exquisite honeypot? Was it not awfully exciting when it throbbed?' Dizzy and bubble headed as Emily was with such overfill draughts of pleasure, she still layed, pronely stretched out, in a delicious lassitude diffused over all her limbs, hugging herself for being thus reprisal to her heart's content. She should have held it ingratitude to the pleasure she had received, to have repented of it.

After feeling well recovered from the delighted sex session she'd received she took care to have a warm bath of redolent and sweet herbs; it was not without some alarm and uneasiness that the fine young Emily thought of what change that tender, soft venus of hers might have sustained, from the shock of a manhood so sized for its dismantle. But beautiful Emily was soon pleasingly cured of her fears. In which having fully soothed herself, she came out sensually refreshed in body and mind. For the pleasures of love had been to them both, what the joy of victory is to a host: renewal, revitalizing, the whole lot.

They had discovered that mutual handlings gave a certain amount of pleasing sensation; and, just now, beautiful Emily had discovered that the hooding and unhooding of Michael's broad manhood, as she called it, instantly caused it to swell up and stiffen as hard as a piece of plank. Michael's feeling of her little pinky slit gave rise in her to nice sensations, but on the slightest attempt to insert even his middle finger, the pain was too great. The session had made so much progress in the wild adventures that not the slightest inkling of what could be done in that way dawned upon them. Michael had always seemed to develop a slight growth of moss-like curls round the root of his manhood; and then, to their surprise, they were perfectly innocent of guile and quite habituated to let each other look at all their naked bodies without the slightest hesitation.

Chapter 4

When he first settled in the lush parts of Castries, Michael Chivers's interest in women was prudently confined by necessity. He was almost twenty two, a very smart deceiving twenty one. His desire toward the opposite sex was as strong as any man's; growing even stronger, perhaps, because of the successes that lay behind him. But he was carrying light, as the saying is. He had looked around comprehensively and carefully before choosing this part of the city as a permanent base of operations, and his cashflow was now reduced to less than four thousand dollars.

That wasn't a lot of money, of course. Unlike the big-con operator, whose intricate scene-setting may involve as much as two hundred thousand dollars, the short-con grifter can run on small change. But Michael Chivers, while remaining resolute to the short con, was abandoning the normal strategy of things.

At twenty one, he was exhausted from the small time swindle. He knew that the regular cheating from one community to another before the heat got too hot, could draw in most of the heists, even of a man who shows careful use of money. So that he might work as hard and often as he safely could, and still wind up with the laws of the land nipping at the seat of his threadbare pants.

Michael had seen such men.

Once, at Joe's bar. A bar on the outskirts of Dennery there were two men who just won a loot on a card game.

The approach of one of the two men was something like the sideways waddle of an aged crab whose eyes looked to the east, but his legs took him to the south. He was stern of face, with an arched, cruel nose, gleaming cast eyes, heavy, straight brows which pointed up and gave a touch of the lion look to his expression, a narrow, jutting chin, and lips habitually compressed to a thin line. It was a handsome face, in a way, but it showed such a brutal dominance that it inspired fear first and admiration afterward.

Such a man must command. He might be a gambler, but never in any case an underling. Altogether, he combined physical and intellectual strength to such a degree that both men and women would have stopped to look at him, and once seen he would be remembered.

The other man wore a pimp coloured hat tipped with an air of challenge over his eyes. Between his teeth, an expensive cigar stump was tilted at the angle of rebellion. He walked with a certain swing of the shoulders which horrified the fearful. His face was rugged, his eyes were piercing brown like those of a hunting eagle. He was singing to the song playing, his voice was deep and easy-on-the ear. He also had a ragged telephone-shaped scar on his left jaw. He picked up the glass of Jack Daniels, took a long swig from it and belched before he spoke to his compatriot.

A slim curvy brunette hair woman was dancing on a podium. At times she would wiggle her body rapidly like any electric eel or jellyfish, at times she would wiggle slowly like a poaching snake. Depending on the rhythm of the music playing.

Michael and Emily who were sitting in the VIP section of the bar decided to cheat the two men of their winnings.

Emily approached the two men and briefly interrupted them by gracefully gliding towards them, her clothing was always impeccably clean, her perfume filled the air. 'Why don't you two finish your drink with me upstairs in one of the private rooms?' She suggested. 'I promise that you will have a jolly good time with what's on offer'. Seeing her charisma and charm and a pair of finest, well shaped breasts their eyes have seen in a long time, which would make any man's cold heart become warm. Their cruel looking dry eyes instantly became moist, they both shook his heads in pleasant visions of her beauty. Finding it hard to resist the temptation, one of them ordered the most expensive bottle of champagne. And the bar staff had the decency to wipe his nose picking hand on his shirt and apron before he served them. The change, plus extra cash notes from the man's wallet, was to give it to the bar staff to buy a few packs of handkerchiefs, in the hope that he might keep his finger out of his nose.

They reach upstairs in one of the private rooms. Michael shut himself up in the room and hid in the bathroom for some seconds to give his brains a chance to study out certain things in connection with how he would robbed these two men of their loot, as well as to commit the approach of the attractive Emily to the two gamblers wondering if the trick he and Emily played would pay off. Almost any man can be trapped by a woman's beauty, but it takes intellect to outwit a street wise mugger like him.

So intent was the two men on Emily's beautiful body, that they did not notice when the bathroom door swung open, Then Michael said:

'Shut the door and lock it, and leave honey I've got this!

I don't intend to leave until your heart stops beating' Said the scarf-faced man

Michael was quick to react like the speed of a lizard's tongue and whirled about, picking up one of the tea cups on the side table.

The two men named Dean and Bob started to make their fighting move, and Dean was taking out a small knuckle duster from his coat in a very significant manner, while Bob was hastily clenching his fist.

There was trouble brewing in the air

Michael did not wait to be attacked. He made a flying leap at Dean, caught the fellow with his strong powerful arms and flung him clean across the bed, so that his head was rammed against the wall with a thud that seemed to shake the room. And smashed the bottle of champagne on his head. Blood squeezed from his head and trickled down the gnarled cheeks.

Then Michael went towards Bob, you son of a bitch.

Bob turned to meet him, but did not get round quickly enough.

Michael at six feet five inches tall, with the muscular shoulder of a rugby player, slammed him up against the wall so that it nearly dented it.

'Glad you gentlemen called,' Michael declared, gently. 'Make yourselves at home. I shall do my best to entertain you.'

He swung a hard upper cut on Bob's chin. Then put him in a headlock, and gave his neck a hard squeeze.

'Wow!' cried Bob 'I didn't come up to fight with you!'

'I know you didn't?'

'What.'

'Gimme the loot you two just won off the card game son-of-a-bitch'

'What? It's only eight thousand'

'I don't care how much it is you son of a bitch'

He caught Bob by the slack of his trousers and the collar and thumped his hard knuckle straight into his throat.

Bob's body fell on the bed, his heels stuck out, and there he lay.

Dean was raving mad. He literally frothed at the mouth as he got off the bed and leaped towards Michael.

'I'll kill you!' he howled.

'Will you?' Michael inquired, calmly. 'I don't think so, you son of a bitch!'

Seeing that Michael was determined to take their winnings, Dean and Bob decided to give up the fight and handed Michael the cool sum of eight thousand dollars.

The music and other entertainment was so loud in the bar that the customers kept on having fun, oblivious to the commotions that just happened upstairs.

As Emily and Michael pulled out of the bar. Michael saw them standing on the door entrance, shoulders hunched against the cool night air, naked fear on their pale, gaunt faces. And in the warm comfort of Emily's car, he shivered for them.

He shivered for himself.

That was where the mugging game landed you, where it could land you. This, or something more dangerous than this, was the fate of the unrooted. Men to whom roots were a jeopardy rather than a resource. And the big scam boys were no more favored to it than their relatively petty brother. In fact, their fate was often worse. Self immolation. Alcohol addiction, The big house and the mental institution.

Emily sat up, swinging her legs off the bed, and got a cigarette from the dressing table. After it was lit, Michael took it for himself, and she got herself another.

'Michael,' she said, 'seriously, look at me.'

'Oh, I am always looking at you, babe. Believe me, I am.'

'Now, please! Is this all the cash we have, Michael? Is it all we're going to have? I'm not knocking it, understand, but shouldn't there be a good few more?'

'How could we crack a thing like that? Michael tickled Emily's feet?'

She looked at him silently, the shining eyes turning dull, staring at him from behind an invisible shield. Without turning her head, she extended a hand and slowly stumped out her cigarette.

'That was funny,' he said. 'You were supposed to laugh.'

'Oh, I am laughing, dear,' she said. 'Trust me, I am.'

She reached down, picked up a jean and began to draw it on. A little bother, Michael pulled her around to face him.

'What are you getting at, Emily? You want a millionaire?'

'I didn't say that.'

'But that's what I asked.'

Emily knit brows, pausing, then shook her head. 'I don't think so. I'm a very pragmatic little girl, and I don't consider giving any more than I get. That might be pretty tricky for a small-time mugger, or whatever you are.'

He was wounded, but Michael kept on playing. 'Would you mind handing me my emergency response kit? I think I've just been hammered.'

'The fact is, the fake lagers are just a sideline. My real business is running a massage parlour.'

Overhead and income were always in a nip and tuck race. One bad deal, and they were on the fall.

And it wasn't going to happen to Michael Chivers.

For his first couple of years moving away from the home he shared with his sister, he was strictly a law abiding citizen. An independent salesman making bath soaps and lagers. Gliding back into the shady deals, he remained a salesman. And he was still one now. He had built up his credit rating and a bank account. He was acquainted directly with hundreds of people who would vouch to the excellence of his character.

Sometimes they were required to do just that, when suspicion threatened to build into a law enforcement officer matter. But, naturally, he never called upon the same ones twice; and it didn't happen often anyway. Safety gave him confidence, and assurance. Safety and confidence, and assurance had bred a high degree of skill.

In achieving so much, he had had no time for settling down just yet. Nothing but the casual main squeeze contacts which any young person might have. It was not until late in his second year at the Park Royal that he had started looking around for a particular kind of woman. Someone who was not only highly decent, but who would be willing to accept the only kind of arrangement which he was willing to offer.

He found her, Emily Casey, in the shopping mall.

Michael was a little stunned to find such a one as Emily Casey present. She just wasn't the type. He was aware of her bemusement when she saw him, but he had his reasons for being there. It was an innocent way of passing the time. Cheaper than posh expensive restaurants and twice as nice. Also, while he was doing very well as it was, he was not blind to the possibility of doing better. And a man just might see a way to do it at gatherings like these.

The audiences were axiomatically knockers. Mostly wealthy ladies knockers, middle-aged working class and spinsters. Oh well, you never knew, did you?

You could keep your eyes open, without going out on an arm.

The shoppers finished their shoppings. Baskets were passed for the 'shop assistants to stock up.' Emily tossed her shopping in one of them, and walked out. Smiling, Chivers followed her.

She was lingering in the lobby, making a business out of pulling on her gloves. As he approached, she looked up with cautious consent.

'Now, what,' he said, 'what's a nice girl like you doing in a place like this store?'

'Oh, you know.' She laughed lightly. 'I just dropped in for some blouses.'

'Looking down his nose. It's a good thing I didn't offer you a hand with your basket.'

'It certainly is. I won't settle for less than some moncler tops.'

They took it from there.

It took them rapidly to where they were now. Or reasonable copy thence.

Lately, today in particular, he sensed that she wanted it to take them somewhat further.

There was just one way of handling that, in his opinion. With the light touch. No one could at the same time laugh and be serious.

He let his hand walk down her body and come to rest on her tummy. 'You know something?' he said. 'If you put a strawberry jam on that, you could pass as a sweet doughnut.'

'Don't,' Emily said, picking up his hand and dropping it to the bed.

'Or you could draw a ring around it, and pretend you're a ring doughnut.'

'I'm beginning to feel like a doughnut,' she said. 'The part in the centre.'

'Oh, fine. I was afraid it might be something immoral.' Then, cutting him off sternly, pulling him back into line, 'But you see what I'm driving at, Michael. We don't know a lot about each other. We're not friends. We're just acquainted. It's just been early to bed and early to bed since the time we met.'

'You said you weren't knocking it.'

'I'm not. It's very important to me. But I don't feel that it should begin and end with that. It's like trying to live on salad and fruits.'

'And you want prawn cocktails?'

'Ribeye Steak. Something nourishing. Aah, hell, Michael' she shook her head agitatedly. 'I don't know. Maybe it isn't on the menu. Maybe I'm in the wrong eatery or apartment.'

'Senorita is too cruel! They will drown themself in the soup!'

'Senorita doesn't care,' she said, 'if senorita lives or dies. He's made that pretty clear.'

She started to rise, with a certain decisiveness of movement. He caught her and pulled her back to the bed, pulled her body against his again. He felt for her carefully. He smoothed her hair and kissed her tasty lips.

'Mmm, yes,' he said. 'Yes, I'm sure of it. The sale is final, and there are no exchanges.'

'Here we go again,' she said. 'Out into outer space, before we have our feet up the ladder.'

'I mean, I went to a great deal of trouble to find you. A very nice little chick. Perhaps there are better chicks in the city, but again there might not be. And--'

'--and a sexy chick in bed is better than a shrub. Or something. I'm afraid I'm crabbing your sermon, Michael.'

'Wait babes!' He held onto her. 'I'm trying to tell you something. That I like you and that I'm slothful. I don't want to look any further. So just show me the scheme, and if I can! I will buy into it.'

'That's better. I have an idea it might be quite money-spinning for both of us.'

'So where do we begin? A few evenings in the town? A project at Castries?'

'Mmm, no, I guess not. Besides, you couldn't afford it.'

'Surprise,' he said sharply. 'I wouldn't even make you pay your own way.'

'Now, Michael . . .' She played with his hair fondly. 'That isn't the kind of thing! I have in mind, anyway. A lot of senoritas, glitter and glassware. If we're going to some place, it ought to be at the other end of the road. You know. Relaxed and quiet, so that we can talk for a change.'

'Well. well it's nice this time of year.'

Toward the town the sky was banked with golden clouds, while the earth revealed the same colors in the yellow earth. Never were skies bluer, never did the golden sunrise flood steep of the large town in richer life-giving glory. A few birds swerved before the meeting, their wings fluttered, and they illuminate on branches of trees and shyly eyed each other, squirrels peeping from their lairs. Did a man need to have the still message of all their ways to summed up in final emphasis, this it was: a beautiful day is here.

'It's always Jolla nice any time of year. But are you sure you can afford--'

'Keep it up,' he warned her. 'One more word of that song, and you'll have the shiniest legs in Castries. People will think it's another sunset.'

'Wooh! Who's afraid of you?'

If she hadn't suspected anything, she wouldn't have noticed it at all. As it was, she smiled at him, and her smile may have said it all.

Because now his grip caught hold of her, and was a little tighter, but still over her blouse. She moved closer to him between his open knees, he didn't fight her off, just kept smiling. Then Michael suddenly became crimson red in the face, pulled Emily close, kissed her passionately, picked up her dress and played with her split with his fingers. And at the same time licking one of her breast nipples. But it was a completely contrasting game than he had ever known before. Emily was sure he was playing with one finger, she felt as if she was in an earthly paradise, as if he was probing her deeply even though he wasn't and she began to move slowly while she was leaning on his chest. Michael took her by the hand and led her, and she was holding on to his strong arms. When she saw his huge, broad manhood, she quickly clasped her hands with joy. She, however, instantly used her soft hands and stroked up and down his broad pole and he played with her breasts and kissed her. So they rubbed each other for a while until their bodies were completely warm.

The movements of Emily's beautiful form were most graceful and enchanting, and one leg being thrown backwards left her lovely honey pot full in view, and actually gaping open before Michael. Michael looked at Emily's clitoris, and it was the site of the most exquisite sensation; he could see it is rather hard, even now, but he will find as he titillates it with his fingers, that it will become harder and more projecting, so applied his middle finger there. Michael soon found her clitoris stiffen and stood up nearly half an inch longer.

The convulsive twitches of Emily's buttocks, the pressure forward of her hand on his head, all proved the exquisite felicity Michael's lovely lover was enjoying. He slipped his hand under his jawline, the position was awkward, but he managed to thrust his thumb into her honeypot. His forefinger was somewhat in the way, but finding it a rosy hole of her honeypot, and all being very moist there, he pushed it forward and it slowly entered. Michael could not move his hand very actively, but he continued to gently draw his finger and thumb a little back together, and then thrust forward again. It seemed to add immensely to the pleasure he was giving her; her whole body quivered with excessive excitement. His head was pressed so firmly against her breast that he had difficulty in breathing, but he managed to keep up the action of tongue on the breast and fingers in the honeypot until he brought on the exquisite crisis, her backside rose, her hand pressed hard on his head and her two powerful and fleshy thighs closed on his fingers on each side and gripped the fingers as if in a vice, while she wiggled her honeypot around in circles, she had so much movements of enjoyment, hardly knowing what she was doing. As she held him so fast in every way, he continued to lick her breast, and continued at the same time to pass his finger over her pouty lips. This, by producing a new excitement, brought her senses round. So relaxing her hold of him with her thighs she moans.

'Oh, my sugar plum Michael, come to my arms so that I may kiss you for the exquisite delight you have given me.' Michael did so, but took care, in drawing himself slowly to her lips, to engroove his very hard, stiff-standing manhood in the well-moistened open honeypot that lay raised on a pillow so conveniently in the way.

Michael shut Emily's mouth with his kisses and tongue, and soon the active movements he was making within her charming honeypot exercised their usual influence on her lubricity, so as to make her as eager for the fray as himself.

He decided to lick her nipples once more before getting into more serious actions. He was so delighted to look at the prominence pouting lips of her tiny slit, all was most promising and charming. He stooped and frigg Emily's little prominent clitoris with his middle finger; it instantly hardened, and she gave a convulsive twitch of her groins.

'Oh! Michael, how nice it is! Oh, I beg you to go on. Oh, how nice!'

Michael always remained serious and calm. He grabbed her hindquarters with one hand, pressed her against him so that her back was leaning against the bed-head, and the next moment she moaned heavily because he had suppressed a cry of pleasure. With some, superbly skillful thrusts his dick had penetrated her all the way to the shield. It was a solid manhood, long and very chunky, and he didn't move for a few seconds after he put it in her honey pot. Then he made short hard thrusts against her, but without pulling his machine out even an inch. He stuck inside her honeypot like a glue and she was half senseless with lust. Then he started drilling again as if he wanted to pummel her split, but he always got stuck deep inside. That hadn't happened to her, this was the first in her lifetime. She groaned tenderly because she was climaxing. Before she had time to be surprised by this experience, he changed the way he pushed, slowly pulling his manhood all the way out, then slowly plunging it all the

43

way again in her honeypot, but she wasn't at all surprised that such a fine young lad could perform so well.

Michael held her medium size nipples, moistened his fingertip, and played with them softly as if with a licking tongue. Swift and more swiftly, rapid and more rapidly, and soon her nipples, which drove her completely crazy with the tickle. Under this treatment, all her coyness disappeared.

He now held her round, medium size breasts firmer. They stood out like two wan balls and bore the mark as if there were a cherry on each wan ball. Michael was very much a fan of such fresh fruit, because he quickly put one cherry after the other into his mouth and picked them off so that they only became more lustrous, the same way some fruit persons in town lick their cherries with their tongues, to give them an appetizing shine through the saliva.

They had been doing this for a while with lots of huffing and panting, Michael said: 'Does it feel nice.?'

'Yes,' Emily replied, 'that feels so nice'

Michael lifted his head from her breast and asked her again : 'Are you enjoying this?'

Shaking with desire and wanting more, Emily quickly said: 'Yes, Michael.' He ran his tongue again over her breasts, so softly that the pleasure was both intense and exciting.

He now started to work on her clitoris. She felt as if everything that was sensation was suddenly down there, mouth, tits. The honey juice flowed from her and soaked the tip of his moist middle finger that passionately touched her, electricity seemed to shoot into her entire body. She lost her breath, the room spun with her, and she closed her eyes.

Michael was once again fucking like a robot constantly on charge. His bottocks flew up high and sank low. But because Emily hugged him tightly with her legs, she was torn up and down by every thrust, and the whole bed shook under this vibration.

She then changed position and slowly lowered herself onto his manhood so that it penetrated as deeply as possible, then she raised herself, and inclining closer to him, she put her breasts in his hand, which he could feel very well with his broad hands. He compressed them softly and indiscernible stroked the nipples that had been erected.

It was very good the way Michael did it. With one hand, which he placed on Emily's back, he pressed her against him, with the other hand he moved around her breasts, and at the same time he kissed her on the mouth so gently and tenderly that she was completely touched by it.

Once again he took her breasts in his mouth and sucked softly. He did it so tenderly, so slowly, that she came instantly. He continued to suck her breasts and she was about to feel bliss for the second time when his toungue slipped away from her powerlessly.

They decided to take a break, shower, and they had a very healthy meal, and the tableware was removed, and left in the dishwasher to do its work.

They both sat on one of the large sofas laid by some fancy design looking cushion, watching music videos on the Television. Never, however, did dear young man carry in his head more wherewith to explain the turning of a girl's head, and making her set all consequences at defiance, for the sake of following a lionhearted.

For, besides all the perfections of manly beauty which were assembled in Michael's form, he had an air of neatness and elegance, certain smartness in the carriage and port of his head, that yet more distinguished him; his eyes were sprightly and full of meaning; his looks had in them something at once sweet and imperious; his complexion out-bloomed the lovely coloured rose, whilst its unique tender graphic glow clearly saved it from the reproach of wanting life, of raw and riches, which is regularly made of those so extremely fair as he was.

The sight, the touching, the being, if but for a day or night, with this idol of Emily's fond virgin heart, appeared to her a happiness above the purchase of her life. He might use her still, let him: he was the master, happy, too happy, even to receive him like a conquering lion when they meet its prey. To this purpose were the reflections of her past couple of hours, of which every minute seemed to her a little eternity.

Emily's eyes were instantly filled with water, but waters of the most delicious delight; to find herself in the arms of that beauteous young man Michael, was a cloud nine that her little glean swam in; past or future were equally out of the question with her; the present was as much as all her powers of life were sufficient to bear the transport of, without fainting. Not either were the most tender embraces, the most soothing expressions wanting on his side, to assure her of his love, and of never giving her cause to repent the bold step she had taken, in throwing herself consequently entirely upon his honor and kindness. She was driven to it by a passion too impulsive for her to resist, and both of them did what they did, because they could not help it.

Michael was a greedy young man when it came to love making, he had just allowed the meal to settle for no more than half of an hour, he came running, caught Emily in his arms, and lifting her from the sofa, with his lips glued to hers, she was shivering, panting, dying with soft fears and tender wishes, to the bed; where his impatience would not suffer him to undress her casual shirt she was wearing, he decided to leave her panty on for a while.

Her bosom was now bare, and rising in the warmest throbs, presented to his sight and feeling the firm hard swell of a pair of young breasts, such as may be imagined of a young woman, fresh out of the country, and never before handled: but even their pride, trend, pleasing resistance to the touch, could not bribe his restless hands from wandering; but, giving them the loose, her panty were soon peeled off, and the lovely center of attraction laid open to his tender incursion. By the very touch of his hand insinuated her thighs to be opened a way for the main attack.

For the moment, Emily laid fairly exposed to the examination of Michael's eyes and hands, quiet and compliant; which confirmed him the opinion he proceeded so proudly upon, that she was no novice in these matters.

Being now too high wound up to keep up any waiting period, Michael's manhood swung from near his thighs, and his engine of love assaults hoisted vigorously. He now resumes his attempts in more form: first, he put two of the pillows under her, to give the blank of his aim a more favorable elevation, and another under her head, in ease of it; then spreading her thighs, and placing himself standing between them, made them rest upon his.

He decided to change the position this was to ensure Emily would feel his hard machine so far inside her, she would feel it up to her belly-button. Michael asked Emily to lay down on her side, and lift up her right leg over his hips, then placed her left thigh between his thighs, then slightly twisting her bottom up towards him brought the lips of her honeypot directly before his solid manhood, which she seized with her delicate fingers, and guided safely into the altar of love. He gave her a few hard shoves, and she a heave or two, applying then the point of his broad hard manhood to the split, into which he sought entrance; it was so tiny, he could rarely assure himself of its being rightly pointed. He looks, he feels, and satisfies himself: there pumping on with fury, its mammoth stiffness, thus impacted, wedgelike, breaks the union of those parts, and gained him just the fitting of the tip of it, lip deep; which being sensible of, he improved his advantage, and following well his pump, in a straight line, powerfully deepens his penetration; she felt a sharp pain, from the separation of the sides of that soft passage by a stiff thick body, she almost screamed out; but, as she was unwilling to alarm the event, she held in her breath, and stuffed a part of a pillow case which was;

turned up over her face, into her mouth, and bit it through in the pain. At length, the soft texture of that tract giving way to such fierce ripping and grueling, he pierced further into her: and now, outrageous and no longer his own manhood, but braced headlong away by the fury and fearlessness of that member, now exerting itself with a kind of native rage, he breaks in, carries all before him, and gave several more violent, merciless thrusts.

When she recovered her senses, she found herself in the arms of the sweet relenting Michael performing like a conquering lion of Judah. He continued slowly and hard ramming in and out of her juicy sheath, Michael find his manhood still lightly held within the velvety folds of one of the most delicious honeypot ever created for the felicity of man, She could not refuse his warm hugs; her eyes, however, moistened with tears, and weakly turned facing him, seemed to reprove him with his cruelty, and ask him, if such were the rewards of his love. Michael employed himself with so much sweetness, so much warmth, to sooth, to caress, and comfort Emily in her soft complainings, which breathed, indeed, more love than resentment, that she presently drowned all sense of pain in the pleasure of seeing him, of thinking that she belonged to him: he who was now the absolute hero of her happiness, and, in four words, her knight in shining armor.

For Michael's good essence to put his patience presently to another trial; but as Emily could walk across the room, he ordered more wine to be brought to the apartment, where it could not be otherwise than them getting down the wing of a bird, and several more glasses of wine, since it was Michael's the cherished young man who both served, and urged them on her, with that sweet irresistible authority with which love had invested him over her.

Michael when lifting up his own shirt and he laid his naked glowing body to her, oh insupportable delight! oh! superhuman rapture! what pain could stand before a pleasure so transporting? She felt no more the smart of her split below; but, curling round Michael like the stem of a climbing plant, as if she feared any part of him should be untouched or unpressed by her, she returned his strenuous embraces and kisses with a zeal and flurry only known to true love, and which mere lust never rise to.

Yes, even at this time, that all the absolute powers of the passions will soon be over, and that her veins roll no longer but a cold calm stream, the remembrance of those passages that most affected her in her prime, still cheers and refreshes her. Her beauteous Michael was now glued to her in all the folds and twirls that they could make their bodies meet in; when, no longer able to rein in the fierceness of refreshed desires, he gives his manhood the leading position, and gently slipping his thighs between hers, stopping her mouth with kisses of humid fire, makes a fresh explosion, and renewing his thrusts, pierces, tears, and forces his way up the well formed tender folds, that gave him entrance with a modish little less severe that when the break was first made she choked, however, her cries, and bore him with the submissive resilience of an heroine; soon his thrusts, more and more furious, cheeks flushed with a deeper ruby, his eyes turned up in the fervent fit, some dying suspires, and an agonizing tremble, announced the approaches of that ecstatic pleasure, she was yet in too much pain to come in for her share of.

Not until after a few enjoyments had callous and blunted the sense of the smart, and given her to feel the titillating drawing in breath of soothing sweets, drew from her the delicious return, and brought down all her passion, that she arrived at surplus of pleasure through superfluous of pain. But, when successive sessions had smashed and hardened her, he began to enter into the true steadfast relish of that pleasure of pleasures, when his machine drilled through all the ravished inwards; what floods of joy that touched her! what agonies of delight! too fierce, too mighty for species to sustain? Well has she therefore, no doubt provided the relief of a delicious momentary wildness, the approaches of which are revealed by a dear delirium, a sweet thrill, on the point of emitting those elation, in which enjoyment itself is drowned, when one gives the weak stretch out.

How often, when the rage and rumpus of their senses had subsided, after the frenzied time, have they, in a tender meditation, asked themselves cooly the question, if it was in the cosmos for any of its creatures to be so happy as they were? Or, what were all fears of the reaction, put in the scale of several hours of enjoyment, of anything so transcendently the taste of their eyes and heart, as that delicious, fond, peerless couple.

Thus they spent the whole afternoon, until supper time in a continued circle of love delights, kissing, chocolates on the breasts, toying, and all the rest of the feast. At length, supper was ordered from a fancy restaurant that provided delivery services.

After having a shower together, Michael ate most of it. He slipped his boxers on; and sat down by the table with huge amounts of food. He ate with a very good appetite, and seemed charmed to see Emily eat as well. For her part, she was so transported with the comparison of the delights she now swam in, with the inane of all her past stages of life, that she thought them sufficiently reasonable. The present possession was all her cute head could find room for.

They lay together that night, when, after playing repeated prizes of hugs and soft kisses, the universe, lavishness and satisfaction, gave them up to the arms of sleep: those of her dear Michael encircled Emily, the consciousness of which made even their sleep more delicious.

Chapter 5

When they woke early the next morning, they had been asleep for at least eight hours; the sleep sunk so deep in slumber after fitful naps that the return to earth was a slow, scarcely credible process. A soothing, rhythmic sweep of sound seemingly saying, 'Sleep on, Sleep on'; but a song sparrow perched on the corner above the window was loudly declaring that it was ecstasy to waken. The rapturous burst, often repeated, won their slow attention. The sun shone through the rosy curtains and a breeze fanned both their opening eyes.

It was a beautiful morning; the air was delightfully fresh and cool, and the rays of the sun danced and glistened upon the dew-drops which sparkled upon every tree and flower. The feathered songsters filled the air with their sweet tunes, and nature with all its cheerful beauty was spread before him. Such a feeling of rest and thorough enjoyment came over Michael, that it was with effort, he was able to shake off the pleasures of the hour.

Emily showered and kissed Michael a hard long kiss. She left, smiling smugly. Very pleased with herself.

Michael arose weakly, his legs shaking as he made the round trip to the bathroom. He dropped back down on the bed in a heap, a little worried about himself for the first time. What could be the cause of this, anyway, this strange overpowering tiredness? Not Emily, surely; he was used to her. Not the fact that he had been screwing and eating very little during the past few days. He often had spells when he didn't feel hungry, and this had been one of them. Whatever he ate bounced back, in a liquid. Which was strange, since he'd eaten nothing but curry and rice last night.

Frowning, he leaned forward and examined himself. There was a faint purplish bruise on his arm. But it didn't hurt any more--unless he pushed on it very hard. He'd had no pain since the night he was fighting Bob and Dean.

So---? He hurtled and lay back down. It was just one of those things, he guessed. He didn't feel sick. If a man was ill, he felt ill.

He piled the pillows on top of one another, and reclined in a half-sitting position. That seemed to be better, but tired as he was he was restless. With an effort, he reached his trousers from a nearby chair, and dug twenty bucks from the pocket.

Offhand, it looked like any other twenty dollar note, but it wasn't quite. The tail side was worn down, the head was not. Holding it back between the fleshy part of his first two fingers, hidden edgewise by them, he could point out the two sides.

He flipped it into the air, caught it and brought it down against his other hand with a whack. For this was the whack, one version of it. One of the three standard short-con gimmicks.

'Heads,' he murmured, and there were heads.

He tossed the note again, and called for tails. And tails came up.

He began closing his eyes on the calls, making sure that he wasn't unconsciously cheating. The note went up and down, his palm deceptively whacking the back of his hand.

Heads ... tails ... heads, tails . . .

And then there was no whack.

His eyes closed, and stayed closed.

That was a little after midday. When he opened them again, the sun ray was warming the room and the phone was ringing. He looked around wildly, not recognizing where he was, not knowing where he was. Lost in a world that was as weird as it was startling. Then, moving slowly back into awareness, he picked up the phone.

'Yes,' he said; and then, 'What, what? How's that again?' For what the reception was saying made no sense at all.

'A visitor, Mr. Michael Chivers. A very attractive young lady. She says'--a tactful laugh--'She says she's your sister.'

Chapter 6

At the age of eighteen, Michael Chivers had left home. He took nothing with him but the clothes he wore, clothes he had bought and paid for himself. He took one hundred and twenty dollars in the pockets of his clothes, and that too he had earned.

He wanted nothing to do with his sister Jasmine Chivers. She had conned him out of his inheritance when he needed it, when he was too young and naive to get for himself, and he wasn't letting her into the game at this late date.

He had no contact with her during the first year he was away. Then, at Christmas time, he sent her a Christmas wish, and on birthday he sent her a birthday card. Both were of the tacky nostalgic type, flooded with sickly sweetness, but the latter was a real beauty. Hearts and flowers and fat little angels swarmed over it in a deadly, extremely amusing collage. The engraved message was dedicated to Dear parents, and it poured tearfully of goodnight kisses and platters and pitchers of freshly baked cakes and soda pops when a little boy came in from play.

You would have thought that Dear parents, nay their souls rest in internal power had been the proprietor of a combination of acres of lands, farming and serving to a few customers her own little nipper.

Michael was laughing so hard when he sent it that he almost screwed up the address. But afterward, he had some clear headed thoughts. He realized perhaps the joke was on him, yes? Possibly by sneering at her he was showing a deep and lasting hurt, admitting that she was tougher than he. And that, needless to say, wouldn't do. She'd taken everything he had to hand out, and it hadn't made a mark in her. Michael definitely mustn't ever let her think that it had.

So he kept in touch with her after that, just to play the field and get back his share of his inheritance. But he was very correct about it. He just didn't think enough of his sister, he told himself, to wallow in ridicule. It would take a lot better woman than Jasmine Chivers to get to him.

The only time he showed his true emotions was in the money making schemes they chose. For while Jasmine could evidently afford far more expensive things than he, he would not admit it. At least, he did not until the effort to keep up with or surpass her not only threatened his long term plans, but exposed itself for what it was. Another revelation of hurt. She had hurt him, or so it clearly looked, and immaturely he was declining her attempts at restitution.

Jasmine might think that, anyway, and he couldn't let her. So he had contacted her casually that out doing each other had been over exploited, and that they should stick to emblematic things, remembrances from then on. If she wanted to run more night clubs, fine. The fast money spinning ones in town would be suitable. He, of course, won't be spending any money in her night clubs.

Well, but that is getting ahead of the tale, leaping over its main element.

Castries is a half-hour ride from Dennery. At eighteen, Michael went there, the logical objective of a young man whose only assets were good looks and an inherent yearn for the quick bucks.

Needing to earn money and to be paid quickly, he took work selling on a flat commission. Door to door goods. Cheap lager, bath soaps, kitchenette devices, and any other items that looked optimistic. All of it promised so much, however he received so little.

Perhaps Kevin of Dennery had made five thousand dollars in his first month by showing Super bed sofas to his friends, and perhaps Jackson of Marigot earned five hundred dollars a day by taking orders for the scuba diving lessons. But Michael doubted it like hell. By literally knocking himself out, he made as high as eight hundred dollars in one week. But that was his very best week. The average was between four hundred and eight hundred dollars, and he had to work hard to get that.

Still it was better than working as a gofer, or taking some small office job which promised a lucky chance and possibility of promotion in lieu of an attractive wage. Promises were cheap. Suppose he went to one of those places and promised to be chief executive officer some day; so how about a little advance?

The selling was no good, but he knew of nothing else. He was very annoyed with himself. Here he was twenty going on twenty one, and already a proven lack of success. What was wrong with him, anyway? What had his sister Jasmine had that he didn't have?

Then, he stumbled into the twenties.

It was a twist of faith. The fall guy, the landlord of a convenience store, had really pulled it on himself. Preoccupied, Michael had continued to fumble for cash after receiving the change from the bill, and the restless storekeeper, delayed in waiting on other customers, had suddenly lost patience.

'For crying out loud, man!' he snapped. 'It's only two dollars! Just pay me the next time you're in.'

Then, he threw back the fifty, and Michael was a block away before he realized what had happened.

On the heels of the realization came another: an ambitious young man did not wait for such happy accidents. He created them. And he, there and then started to do so.

He was sadly told off at a few places. At the others, it was pointed out more or less amiable that he was not entitled to the return of his twenty. At the remaining few others, he collected.

He was elated at his good luck. And he had been extremely lucky. He wondered if there were any ploys similar to the twenties, ways of picking up as much money in a few hours as a blockhead made in a week.

There were. He was introduced to them one night in a bar, whence he had gone to celebrate.

A customer sat down next to him, cannon into his elbow. A little of his drink was spilled, and the man apologetically insisted on buying him a fresh one. Then he bought still another round. At this time, of course, Michael wanted to buy a round. But the man's attention had been rerouted. He was peering down at the floor, then reaching down and picking up a dice cube which he laid on the bar.

'Did you drop this, comrade? No? Well, look. I don't like to drink so fast, but if you want to roll me for a round just to keep things even . . .'

They rolled. Michael won. Which normally wouldn't do at all. They rolled again, for the price of five drinks, and this time the guy won. And, of course, that wouldn't do either. He just wouldn't allow it. What the hump they were just swapping drinks, friendly like, and he certainly wasn't going to walk out of here winner.

'We'll roll for seven drinks this time, well, call it a hundred bucks even, and then . . .'

The knock, with its rapidly doubling bets, is murder on a halfwit. That is its fierce beauty. Unless he is carrying very heavy, the man with the best of it empties him on a relatively innocent number of winning rolls.

Michael's Scamming ways were down the drain within fifteen minutes.

In another fifteen, all of his honest banknotes had followed it. The guy felt very bad about it; he said so himself. Michael must take back a couple bucks of his loss.

But the taste of the cheater was strong in Michael's mouth, the taste and the smell. He said sternly that he would take back half of the cash. The con artist who named Oliver could keep the other half for his services as an instructor in defrauding.

'You can start the lessons right now,' he said. 'Start with that dice stunt you just worked on me.'

There were some resentful protests from Oliver, some strong language from Michael. But in the end they prorogued to one of the booths, and that night and for some nights afterward they played the roles of lecturer and student. Oliver held back nothing. On the contrary, he talked almost to the point of becoming exhausted. For this was a glorious chance to drop falsehood. He could show how smart he was, as his existence usually rules out doing, and do it in absolute safety.

Oliver did not like the old fashion types. It took a certain atrocious thing which he did not have. And he never worked it without an associate, someone to distract the fool while the play was being made. As for working with an ally he didn't like that either. It cut the winning score right down the middle. It put a fruit on your head, and handed the other man a handgun. Because scammers, it seemed, suffered an irresistible desire to beat their comrade. There was little celebration in flogging a dunce hell, dunces were made to be caned. But to take an expert, even if it cost you in the long run, ah, that was something to brigtened your dignity.

Oliver liked the hash . It was simple, you know. Most people matched money.

He particularly liked the interknit, whose many virtues were almost beyond listing. Hook a group of guys on that hash, and you had it made for the week.

The weed must always be played on a very restricted surface, a bar or a booth table. Thus, you could not literally roll the chips, although, of course, you emerged too. You jiggled your hand robustly, holding the cuboid on a high point, never wobbling it at all, and then you spun it out, letting it drift and tumble but never turn. If the marks became mistrustful, you shot out of a mug, or, more likely, a glass, since you were in a bar room. But again you did not really shake the dice. You held it, as before, clicking it strongly against the glass in a replicated clatter, and then you spun it out as before.

It took practice, certainly. Everything did.

If things got too warm, the bar staff would often give you a take-out for a good tip. Call you to the phone or say that the law enforcement officers were coming or something like that. Bart staff were chronically fed up with drinkers, unless they were getting big tips. They'd as soon see them fooled as not, if it made them a buck, and unless the guys were their mates.

Oliver knew of many stunts other than the three standards. Some of them promised payoffs exceeding the normal defrauder top of at least one hundred thousand dollars. But these unchangeables required more than one man, as well as reasonable time and proper planning; were, in short, bordering massive scam stuff. And they had one very serious disadvantage: if the dunce tipped, you were caught. You hadn't made a mistake. You hadn't just been unlucky. You'd just had it.

There were two highly imperative details of defrauding which Oliver did not explain to his student. One of them dismissed the clarification. It was a gained trait, something each man had to do on his own and in his own way; meaning, retaining a high degree of silence while remaining in motion. You couldn't disguise yourself, as might be expected. It was more a matter of not doing anything. Of avoiding any quirk, any declaration, anyvoice quality of figure of speech, any posture or motion or walk, anything at all that might be remembered.

Thus, the first unexplained necessity.

Seemingly, Oliver didn't explain the second one because he saw no need to. It was something that Michael must certainly know.

The tutorial ended.

Michael in full swing went to work on the scam. He picked up a handsome wardrobe. He was shifting from a pals small business enterprise. Wallowing himself excessively, he still built up a roll of more than fifty thousand dollars.

Weeks and months passed. Then, one day, when he was eating in a Greek restaurant lunchroom, a law enforcement officer came in looking for him.

Presenting with the landlord, he described Michael to a scammer. He had no photo of him, but he did have a cop artist's reconstruction, and it was a high quality likeness.

Michael could see them looking down his way, as they talked, and he thought fiercely of running. Of beating it back through the kitchen, and on out the back door. Probably the only thing that kept him from running was the frailty of his legs.

And then he looked at himself in the back-counter mirror, and he breathed a chilling sigh of relief.

The day had turned warm after he left the Park Royal, and he'd checked his hat, over-coat and tie in a compartment. Then, only an hour or so ago, he'd got a crew cut hairstyle.

So he changed a great deal. Enough anyway to keep him from being collared. But he was trembling right down to his shoe bottom. He sneaked back to the Park Royal, wondering if he'd ever have the guts to work again. He stayed in the Park Royal until dark, and then he went looking for Oliver.

Oliver was gone from the small holiday flats where he had lived. He'd left just over a month ago, leaving no forwarding address. Michael started hunting for him. By sheer luck, he found him in a bar five streets away.

The defrauder was horrified when Michael told him what had happened. 'You mean you've been working here all this time? You've been working, steady? My God! Do you know where I've been in the last month? At least four places! All the way to the sea coast and back!'

'But why? I mean, Castries is a big city. Why--'

Oliver cut him off impatiently. Marigot wasn't a big city, he said. It just had a lot of people in it, and they were stuffed to the gills into a relatively small area. And, no you didn't help your odds much by getting out of brimful Gros Islet and doing businesses in the other towns. Not only did you keep bumping into the same people, people who worked in Castries and lived in Marigot, and Gros Islet, but you were more noticeable there. Easier to be spotted by the dunces. 'By the way pal, even a blind man could spot you. Look at that haircut! Look at the fancy expensive brogues, and then the three-stone diamond wristwatch! Why don't you wear a designer sun-shade, too, and a mouthful of gold teeth?'

Michael reddened. He asked agitatedly if every city was like this. Did you have to keep hopping from place to place, using up your capital and having to move on just about the time you got to know your way around?

'What do you want?' Oliver snatched. 'Water in your beer? You can normally play a fairly long stand in Castries, because it ain't just one town. It's a city full of towns, loads of them. And with traffic so crammed and a busy transportation system, the people don't mix around like they do in Marigot. But '--he swayed a finger firmly' but that still doesn't mean you can run wild, pal. You're a scammer, see? A mugger. You've got no family and no friends, and no visible means of financial support. And you certainly better not ever forget it.'

'I won't,' Michael pledged. 'But, Oliver . . .'

'Yeah?'

Michael smiled and shook his head, keeping his thoughts to himself. Suppose I did have a home, a regular place of residence? Suppose I had at least four true friends and two acquaintances? Suppose I had a job and-

And there was a knock on the door, and he said, 'Come in, Jasmine,' and his sister came in.

Chapter 7

She didn't seem to have aged a year in the five years since he'd last seen her. He was twenty-two, now, which meant that she was closing near thirty. But she appeared to be in her very early twenties, say about twenty-two. She looked like ..oh my gosh! Like . . . Why, of course! Emily Casey! That was who she reminded him of. You couldn't say that they actually resembled each other; they both had dark shiny hair and about the same size eight, but there was absolutely no facial resemblance. It was more a type similarity than a personal one. They were both members of the same group; women who knew just what it took to preserve and magnify their natural attractiveness. Women who were either endowed with what it took, or spared no effort in getting it.

Jasmine took a seat sheepishly, unsure of her welcome, quickly explaining that she was in Castries on business. 'I'm handling playback money at the dog tracks, Michael. I'll be getting back to Marigot for some business venture as soon as the races are over.'

Michael nodded calmly. The explanation was reasonable. Playback, knocking the odds down on a greyhound by heavy totalizer betting, was common in bigtime bookmaking.

'I'm happy to see you, Jasmine. I'd have been hurt if you hadn't dropped by.'

'And I'm happy to see you, Michael. I--' She looked around the room, leaning forward a little to peep into the bathroom. Slowly, her modesty gave way to a baffled frown. 'Michael,' she said. 'What's this all about? Why are you living in a place like this?'

'What's wrong with it?'

'Stop chafing me! It isn't you, that's exactly what's wrong. Just look at it! Look at those dull harlequin pictures! That's a sample of my brother's taste? Michael Chivers goes for dull.

Michael would have laughed if he hadn't been so weak. The few pictures were his own additions to the decorations. Hidden in their box frames was his grifted dough. Seven hundred and fifty thousand dollars in cash.

He mumbled that he had rented the place as he found it, the best that he could afford. After all, he was just an authorized salesman and . . .

'And that's another thing,' Jasmine Chivers said. 'Few years in this part of town, like this part of Castries, and a bath soap selling job is the best you can do! You expect me to believe that? It's a front, isn't it? This slag heap is a front. You're working an angle, and don't tell me you're not because I wrote the book!'

'Jasmine . . .' His flake out voice seemed to come from miles away. 'Jasmine, mind your own damn business . . .'

She said nothing for a minute or so, recovering from his scolding, reminding herself that he was more a stranger than a brother. Then, half-pleading, 'You don't have to do it, Michael. You've got so much on the ball, so much more than I ever had. You know what it does to a person, Michael.'

67

Michael's eyes were closed. An evident signal to shut up or buzz off. Forcing a smile, she said, Okay, she wouldn't start scolding the minute she saw him.

'Why are you still in bed Michael? Are you ill?'

'Nothing,' he muttered. 'Just . . .'

She came over to the side of the bed. Shyly, she put the palm of her hand to his forehead; let out a startled pant. 'Why, Michael, you're ice cold! What--' Light bloomed over his pillows as she switched on the side lamp. He heard another pant. 'Michael, what's the matter? You're as blue as a simile!'

'Nothing is wrong with me' His lips barely moved. 'No sweat, Jasmine.'

Suddenly, he became very scared. He knew, without knowing why, that he was terminally ill. And with the horrible fear of death was an intolerable sorrow intolerable because there was no one who cared, no one to soothe it. No one, no one at all, to share it with him.

Only one death, Michael? Well, what are you kicking about?

But they can't eat you, can they? They can eliminate you, but they can't eat you.

'Don't!' he cried, his voice pushing up through an overpowering dizziness. 'Don't laugh at me Jasmine'

'I won't! I'm not laughing, sweet! Listen to me, Michael!' She squeezed his hand firmly. 'You don't seem to be sick. No fever or, Where do you hurt? Did someone hit you?'

He didn't hurt. There had been no pain since the day of his slugging.

'Hit . . .' he muttered. 'Few nights ago . . .'

'Several nights ago? How? Where were you hit? What--Wait a minute, sweet Just wait until your beloved sister makes a phone call, and then--'

In what was record time for the Park Royal, she got an outside line. She spoke over the phone, her voice snapping like a belt.

'. . . Jasmine Chivers, doctor. I work for Riley Hilarity Company out on the mains of Castries, and-- _What?_ Don't you brush me off, dude! Don't tell me you never heard of me! If I have to have Ethan Riley call you--! Well, all right then. Let's see how fast you can get over here!'

She slammed down the receiver, and turned back to Michael.

The doctor came, out of breath and looking a little sullen; then, forgetting his wounded dignity, as his eyes drank in the beauty of Jasmine.

'So sorry if I was prompt, Mrs. Chivers. Now, don't tell me this strapping young man is your brother!'

'Never mind that.' Jasmine chopped off his compliments. 'Do something for him. I think he's in a pretty bad way.

'Well, now. Let's just see.'

He moved past her, looked down at the lightened figure on the bed. Quickly, his light manner washed away, and his hand moved swiftly; testing Michael's heart, probing for pulse and blood pressure.

'How long has he been like this, Mrs. Chivers?'-- curtly, not turning to look at her.

'I don't know. He was in bed when I came in about half an hour ago. We talked and he seemed to be okay, except that he kept getting weaker and--'

'I'll bet he did! Any history of pustules?'

'No. I mean, I'm not sure. I haven't seen him in over four years, and-- What's the matter with him, doctor?'

'Do you know whether he's been in any kind of accident or misadventure during the last few days? Anything that might have injured him internally?'

'No . . .' She corrected herself again. 'Well, yes, he was! He was trying to tell me about it. Few nights ago, he was hit in the chest by some taproom drunk, I suppose . . .'

'Any spewing up afterward? Dark-colored?' The doctor jolted down the sheet, nodding menacingly at the sight of the bruise. 'Well?'

'I don't know . . .'

'What's his blood-type? Do you know that?'

'No. I--'

He dropped the sheet, and picked up the phone. As he called for an ambulance, breaking the Park Royal outside call record for the second time that day, he stared at Jasmine with a kind of worried reprove.

He hung up the phone. 'I wish you'd known his blood type,' he said. 'If I could have got some blood into him now, instead of having to wait until he's typed . . .

'Is it . . . He'll be alright, won't he?'

'We'll do all we can. Oxygen will help some.'

'But will he be all right?'

'His blood-pressure is under a hundred, Mrs. Chivers. He's bleeding.'

'Stop it!' Jasmine wanted to scream at him. 'I asked you a question! I asked you if--'

'I'm sorry,' he said evenly. 'The answer is no. I don't think he can live until he gets to the hospital.'

Jasmine swayed. She got hold of herself; drawing herself straight, making her voice strong. And she spoke to the doctor very quietly.

'My brother will be okay,' she said. 'If he isn't, I'll have you incinerated.'

Chapter 8

Layla Harris arrived at the hospital at two in the afternoon, half an hour before the beginning of her shift. The bare thought of being late to work petrified her, and, by coming so early, she could get a discount-priced meal in the staff's cafeteria before going on duty. That was very important to Layla, a good meal at a low price. Even when she wasn't hungry, which was rare, even in this city where no one seemed ever to be hungry, she was always cautiously worried about when she would eat again.

Her blue nurse's uniform was so stiffly starched that it gave off little pops and crackles as she hurried down the marble corridor. Cut overlong, top exudes a sleek elegant fashion, it made her look like a teenager dressed in its ladies clothes; and the skirt and cuffs flared upward at the corners, seeming to set a pattern for her eyes, her mouth, her brows, and the tips of her short bobbed hair. All her features had a cheerful appearing look, and no amount of inner grandeur could conquer it. In fact, the more majestic she was, the more determinedly severe, the greater the effect of suppressed laughter: a teenager playing at being an adult.

Entering the cafeteria, she moved straight to the long serving counter. Blushing self-consciously; careful to avoid looking at anyone who might be looking her way. Several times, here and elsewhere, she had been drawn into joining other diners. And the experience had been sadly tricky. The men, interns and technicians, made jokes which were beyond her limited expression, so that she never knew quite what her feedback should be. As for the other nurses, they were nice enough; they wanted to be friendly. But there was a great gap between them which only time could bridge. She did not talk or think or act as they did, and they seemed to take her ways as an appraisal of theirs.

Layla took a tray and cutlery from the serving counter, and studied the steamy expanse of food. Carefully, weighing each item against the other, she made her selections.

Potatoes and gravy were healthy options. Then the two orders would be perfectly blended , yes? A very good choice.

'The two-order--?' The plump counter woman laughed. 'Oh, you mean a double?'

'A double, yes?'

The woman hesitated, looked around furtively. 'Tell you what, sweetie pie. We'll make it the same price as a single; hmm? I'll just go a little bit heavy with the spoon.'

'You can do this?' Layla's turned-up eyes rounded with amazement. 'It would not cause trouble?'

'For me? Hah! I own this cafe, sweet.'

Layla guessed that that made it all right. It would not be thieving. Her conscience comfortable, she also accepted the few extra sausages which the woman buried beneath her order of frankfurter and gherkins.

She was hesitating at the dessert section, about to decide that she could have an apple crumble in view of her other economies, when she heard the voices back down the line: the plump woman talking to another attendant.

'A few of the staff can really put it away, can't they?'

'When she gets it for nothing, yes. That's how those travelers get ahead.'

Layla froze for a moment. Then, stiffly, she moved on, paying her check and carrying her tray to a table in a distant corner of the room. She began to eat, expertly; forcing down the suddenly tasteless food until it once again became tasteful and helpful.

That was the way one had to do it. To do the best one could, and accept things as they were. Normally, they did not seem so bad after a while; if they were not actually good, then they became so by the goodness of the many things that were worse. Almost everything was relatively good. Eating was better than being deprived of food, living better than dying.

Even assumed friendliness was better than none at all. People had to care, at least a little, to pretend. Her own kindred and kind, immigrants like herself, had not always done that.

She had come to the country under the auspices of relatives, an aunt and uncle who had fled Albania. Now well-to-do, they had taken her into their home and given her probationary status as a daughter. But with certain unstated conditions: that she become one with them, that she live as they lived, without regard to how she had lived before. And Layla could not do that.'

The routine dining, the numerous sets of dishes, each to be used only for a certain kind of food, were almost offensive to her. So much waste in a world filled with want! Vice versa, it seems foolish to fast in the midst of profusion.

She was shocked to find foolishness masquerading as pride, or what she thought of as lack of intelligence: the impassable to a new language, and a new and possibly better way of life. All in all she was frightened by the honorable apartness, sensing in it the seeds of disaster.

Because they were good to her, or meant to be, she tried to be as they were. She was even willing to believe that they were right and that she was wrong. But only trying, willingness, was not enough for them. They accused her of casting aside her faith, one that she could never remember knowing. Their autocracy, in its own way, seemed almost as bad as that she had fled from, and at last, she had had to depart from them.

Life outside the refugee world wasn't easy. The alternative to it often seemed to be a world with quite as many prejudices as the one she had left. But it was not always that way. There were some people who were completely indifferent to what Layla had been; that is, they were indifferent in a critical sense. They, the rare few: Miss Jasmine Chivers was their best example, accepted her for what she was now. And---

She saw Miss. Chivers approached, moving past the other tables with her easy dominance. Hastily, Layla set down her teacup and came to her feet.

'Please sit down, Miss. Chivers. I will get you some tea, yes? Some coffee? Something to grub--'

'Nothing,' Layla smiled, waving her back to her chair. 'I won't be staying at the hospital this afternoon, and I wanted to talk to you before I left.'

'There is something wrong? I--I have done--'

'No, you're doing just fine. Everything's okay,' Jasmine assured her. 'Get yourself some more tea, if you like. There's no hurry.'

'I'd better not.' Layla Shook her head. 'It is almost five, and the other nurse--'

'I'm paying the other nurse, too,' Jasmine said flatly. 'She's working for me, not the hospital. If she doesn't want to work a little overtime for extra pay, she can quit.'

Layla nodded and murmured meekly. This was a side of Miss. Chivers she had never seen before. Jasmine's smile returned.

'Now, just relax and rest easy, Layla. I like your work. I like you. I hope you like me, too--my brother and I.'

'Oh, I do, very much! You have been very nice to me.'

'Why is it that you don't have a regular job? That you're just working extra?'

'Well . . .' Layla hesitated over her answer. 'The hospital, almost every hospital, has its own graduates, its own nurses, and I am not such a graduate. Then, the regular jobs, like in the doctors' offices, they usually want skills that I do not have. Often bookkeeping and shorthand, and--'

'I understand. How do you make out on this special duty work? All right?'

'Well, I do not always make so much,' Layla said firmly. 'It depends on how much work I can get, and that is not always a great deal. And, of course, there are the fees to the nurses' registry. But … Well, it is enough, whatever. When! know more and when I better grasp the english language--'

'Yeah, sure. How old are you, Layla?'

'Twenty six.'

'Oh?' Jasmine was alarmed. 'I wouldn't have thought you were that old.'

'I feel much older, sometimes. Like I had lived forever. But, yes, I am twenty six.'

'Well, it doesn't matter. Any boyfriends? Going steady with anyone? No?' Jasmine thought that was strange too. 'Now, a girl like you must have had plenty of lucky chances.'

Layla shook her head, her rising attributes humorously imposing. She lived in a furnished small studio apartment, she pointed out, and she could not properly receive young men in it. Then, since it was necessary to work whenever she could, and since she worked unsymmetrical hours, it was not possible to plan ahead nor to be sure of keeping a social commitment if any were made.

'Also,' she concluded, redden, 'also, the young men try to do certain things. They--generally, I am extremely embarrassed.'

Jasmine nodded gently, feeling a weird tenderness toward the girl. Here was something, someone, absolutely real and the reality was all to the good. Perhaps, under different situations, she might have turned out as wholesome and honest--and real--as Layla was. But--she shook herself mentally--to hell with that sound.

She was what she was, and thus Michael had become what he was. And there was nothing to be done about her, presuming that she wanted anything done, but perhaps it wasn't too late.

'You're probably curious why I was so snoopy. Inquisitive, I mean,' Jasmine said. 'Well, it's like this. I don't want to cast a spell on my brother by saying that he's going to be okay, but--'

'Oh, I'm sure he will be, Miss. Chivers! I--'

'Don't say it,' Jasmine said smartly, knocking on the wooden top of the table. 'It might bring bad luck. Let's just say that when and if he is able to leave the hospital, I'd like you to go on looking after him for a while. At my home, I mean. Do you think you'd like that?'

Layla nodded enthusiastically, her eyes shining. She'd already had more than two weeks of steady employment with Miss. Chivers, more than she'd ever had before. What a wonderful thing it would be to go on working for her and her pleasant brother, indefinitely.

'Well, that's fine, then,' Jasmine said. 'It's all settled. Now, I've got to run along, but-- Yes?'

'I was just pondering---' Layla hesitated. 'I was pondering if--if Mr. Chivers would want me. He is always very kind, but ---' She hesitated again, not knowing how to say what she meant without sounding impolite. Jasmine said it for her.

'You mean Michael dislikes me. He's against anything I do simply because I do it.'

'Oh, no. I did not mean that. Not exactly, anyway. I was just . . .'

78

'Well, it's close enough,' Jasmine smiled, trying to make her voice light. 'But don't worry about it, love. You're working for me, not him. Anything I do for him is for his own good, so it doesn't matter if he's a little resentful at first.'

Layla nodded, a trifle doubtfully. Jasmine arose from her chair, and began drawing on her gloves.

'We'll just keep this to ourselves for the time being,' she said. 'It's just possible that Michael will suggest it himself.'

'Whatever you say,' Layla talked in hush tones.

They walked to the door of the cafeteria together. Then Jasmine headed toward the lobby entrance, and Layla hurried away toward her patient's room.

The other nurse left as soon as they had checked the chart together. Michael gave Layla a weakly lazy grin, and told her she looked very second-rate.

'You belong in bed, Miss Ellis,' he said. 'I'll give you part of mine.'

'I don't!_' Layla redden furiously. 'You will _not!_'

'Oh, but you do. I've seen girls with that look before. Bed is the only thing that will heal them.'

Layla giggled unwillingly, feeling very evil. Michael told her seriously that she mustn't laugh about such things. 'You'd better behave or I won't kiss you goodnight. Then, you'll be sorry!'

'I will _not!_' Layla blushed and wriggled and giggled. 'Now, you stop _it!_'

Michael stopped the teasing after a minute or two. She was truly embarrassed by it, he guessed, and he wasn't up to much merriment himself.

Slinged from a metal stand on the right side of his bed was a jar of syrupy-looking blood. A tube extended from the upended top of it to a fringe-like needle in his arm. On the left side-of the bed, a similar device dripped saline water into the artery of his other arm. The blood and water had been fed into him thus since his arrival in the hospital. Lying constantly on his back with his arms held flat, he ached almost endlessly, his only relief coming when his body and arms became numb. Sometimes he found himself pondering if life was worth such a price. But the pondering was comical, strictly on the wry side.

He'd had a long look at death, and he hadn't liked the look of it at all.

He was very, very thrilled to be alive.

Now that he was apparently out of danger, however, he did regret one thing--that it was Jasmine who had saved his life. The one person to whom he wished to owe nothing, he now owed everything, a score or obligation he could never repay.

He could worry and squabble the matter in his mind. He could mention his own incredibly tough constitution, an enticing will to live, as the true source of his survival. The doctors themselves had practically said as much, hadn't they? It was scientifically impossible, they'd said, for a man to live when his blood pressure and hemoglobin fell below a certain level. Yet Michael had been well below that level when he arrived at the hospital. Alone, he had been clinging to life on his own before anything had been done for him.

So nothing. He'd needed help fast, and his sister Jasmine had got it for him. Emily hadn't seen his need, he hadn't, no one had but Jasmine. And just where, for that matter, had he got the mental and physical firmness to hold on until he had medical help? From strangers? Huh-uh.

Any way you looked at it, he indebted his life to Jasmine. And Jasmine, unconsciously or deliberately, was making sure that he didn't forget it.

In a nicely kitten fashion, she'd put such ice on Emily Casey that Emily had stopped coming to the hospital after a couple of visits. She called every day, letting him know that she was worried about him, but she didn't come back again. And Jasmine often managed to be on hand at the time of her calls, practically restricting his end of the conversation to the point or short and sweet.

Jasmine obviously intended to break up his affair with Emily. Nor did her intentions end there. She'd selected a day nurse for him who was a real shocker, competent enough but homely as a mud fence. Then, by contrast, she'd picked a beautiful doll for night duty, the sort that was bound to appeal to him even if Jasmine hadn't given her a clear field with no competition.

Oh, he could see what was happening. Everywhere he looked, he could see the shadow of Jasmine's fine hand. And just what could he do about it, anyway? Tell her to get the hell away and leave him alone? Could he say, 'Okay, you saved my life; does that give you any claim on me?'

A doctor came in, not the one who had visited at the Park Royal, Jasmine had dismissed him right at the beginning, but a merry-looking young man. Behind him came an orderly, wheeling a metal-topped cart. Michael looked at the implements on it, and let out a sigh.

'Oh, no! Not that thing again!'

'You mean you don't like it?' The doctor laughed. 'He's joking with us, isn't he, nurse? He loves to have his stomach pumped.'

'Please.' Layla scowled cynically. 'It is not funny.'

'Aah, you can't hurt this guy. Rally round now, and we'll get it over with.'

The orderly held him on one side, one hand clamping over the intravenous needle. Layla held the needle into the other arm, her free hand poised over a bowl of tiny ice cubes. The doctor picked up a narrow rubber tube and pushed it up into his nose.

'Now, hold still, young man. Hold still or you'll wrench those needles loose!'

Michael tried to hold still but he couldn't. As the tube went up into his nose and down into his throat, he tugged and struggled. Gagging, gasping for breath, he tried to break free of them. And the doctor cursed him merrily, and Layla pressed little ice lumps between his lips.

'Please swallow, Mr. Chivers. Swallow the ice and the tube will go down with it.'

Michael kept swallowing. At last the tube was down his throat and into his stomach. The doctor made some minor adjustments in it, moving it up and down slightly.

'How's that? Not hitting bottom, is it?'

Michael said he didn't think so. It seemed to be okay.

'Good.' The doctor checked the glass receptacle to which the pump was attached. 'I'll be back in forty five minutes, nurse. If he gives you any trouble, sock him in the stomach.'

Layla nodded coldly. She looked after him, giving a dirty look, as he strode out of the room, then came over to the bed and patted away the sweat from Michael's face.

'I am sorry. I hope it does not bother you too much.'

'It's okay.' He felt a little shamefaced at the fuss he had made. 'I'm just kind of conscious of it, you know.'

'I know. The worst part is getting it down, but afterward it is not good. You cannot swallow well and your breathing is ever-so-slightly impeded, and never do you become accustomed to it. Always, there is the consciousness of something wrong.'

'You sound like you'd been pumped yourself.'

'I have been, many times.'

'Internal bleeding?'

'No. I began to bleed after a time, but I was not bleeding to begin with.'

'Yes?' he frowned. 'I don't get you. Why were you being pumped out if--'

'I don't know.' She smiled suddenly and shook her head. 'It was a very long time ago. Anyway, it is not pleasant to talk about.'

'But--'

'And I think you should not talk so much, either. You will just lie still, please, and do nothing to disturb your stomach contents.'

'I don't see how there could be any digestive substances.'

'Well, anyway,' she said soundly. And he let it go at that.

It was easy to drop the subject. Easy, in his insistent need to survive, to ignore all possible distractions. Years of practice had made it so easy that it was almost automatic.

Michael lay quietly, watching Layla as she moved about the room, seeing her beautiful freshness as a refreshing relief from Emily. A very nice young lady, he thought, just about as nice as they came. So doubtless she must be left that way. On the other hand, wouldn't it be a little strange if a girl as attractive as she was had remained strictly on the nice side? Weren't the odds all against it? And if she did know the score . . .

Well, it was something to think about. Certainly, it would be a pleasant way of putting Jasmine in her place.

The doctor returned. He checked the glass container of the pump, and chortled happily. 'Nothing but bile. That's what he's full of, nurse, as if you didn't know.'

He removed the stomach tube. Then, wonder of wonders, he ordered the intravenous needles removed from Michael's arms. 'Why not? Why should we baby a cheat like you?'

'Oh, go to hell.' Michael grinned at him, flexing his arms luxuriously. 'Just let me stretch.'

'impertinent, hmm. How about something to eat?'

'You mean that liquid chalk you call milk? Bring it on, brother.'

'Nope. Tonight you get steak, mashed potatoes, and the works. You can even have a couple of cigarettes.'

'You're joking.'

The doctor shook his head, became serious. 'You haven't bled any in a few days. It's time your stomach returns to some peristalsis, starts toughening itself up, and it can't do it on liquids.'

Michael was just a little agitated. After all, it was his stomach. The doctor assured him that he had nothing to worry about.

'If your stomach won't take it, we'll just have to open you up and cut out a piece. No trouble at all.'

He walked out, whistling.

Again, Layla looked after him, knitting her brows. 'That man! Ooh, I would like to wobble him good!'

'You think it will be satisfactory?' Michael asked. 'To have solid food. I mean. I'm not really hungry, and---'

'Of course, it will be good enough! Otherwise, you would not be allowed to have it.'

She took one of his hands in hers, looked down at him so protectively that he wanted to smile. He restrained the impulse, clinging to her hand while he gently urged her into the chair at his side.

'You're a good little nurse,' he said softly. 'I've never known anyone like you.'

'T-thank you.' Her eyes fell, and her voice dropped to a whisper. 'I have known no one like you either.'

He lay studying her in the gathering twilight of the room, examining the small honest face with its tenderly rising features; thinking how much she looked like some greatly innocent child. Then he turned on his side, and eased over near the edge of the bed.

'I'm going to miss you, Layla. Will I see you after I leave here?'

'I--I do not know.' She was breathing heavily, still not looking at him. 'I--I would like to, b-but I must work whenever I can, whenever I am c-called and--'

'Layla?'

'Yes?'

'Come here.'

He drew her forward by the hand, his free hand dropping around her shoulders. She looked up at last, eyes frightened, hanging back desperately. And then, suddenly, she was in his arms, her face pressed against his.

'Like me, Layla?'

'Oh, yes!' her head pulled in assent. 'So, so much! But---'

'Listen,' Michael said. And then as she listened, waiting, he was silent. Putting on the brakes. Telling himself that this was as far as it should go.

But was it? He would need looking after for a while, wouldn't he? Jasmine had hinted at something of the kind, suggesting that he stay in her house for a week or so. He'd been against it, of course, first because it was Jasmine's suggestion, and secondly because it seemed futile. With her away at the tracks and bars so much, he'd still be on his own. But . . .

Layla trembled against him gracefully. He started to shove her away; and, unwillingly, his arms tightened around her.

'I was just thinking,' he said. 'I'll still be a little wobbly after I leave here. Maybe--'

'Yes?' She raised her head, smiled down at him excitedly. 'You would want me to tend to you for a while, yes? That is it?'

'You'd like that?'

'Yes! Oh, my, yes!'

'Well,' he said, stiffly. 'We'll think about it. See what my sister has to say. I live in a holiday apartment myself, so I'd have to stay at her place. And--'

'And it will be just fine!' Her eyes were rocking. 'I know.'

'What do you mean?'

'I mean, it is what your sister wants! I--we were not going to say anything about it yet. She was not sure how you would feel, and--and-_'

Her voice died away under his dull-eyed stare. Swift concern tweaked at the tipped corners of her mouth.

'Please. There is something wrong?'

'Not a thing,' he said. 'No, everything's just fine.'

Chapter 9

The grade A race was over. The trackside crowds surged back through the area which passed beneath the grandstand, and led into the vaulted arena of bars, lunchrooms, and pari-mutuel windows. Some of them were hurrying, smiling broadly, or wearing puff up faces, tight-lipped grins. They headed toward pay-off windows. Others, the majority, came more slowly, scanning their racing programs, tip sheets, and forms; their faces indifferent, desperate, angry, or glum. These were the losers, and some of them went on through the exits to the parking lot, and some stopped at the bars, and most of them moved toward the betting windows.

It was still early in the day. There were still a lot of full pockets. The crowd would not shake out much before the end of the seventh race.

Jasmine Chivers collected five bets at as many windows. Putting the money to one side in her cash register for it would have to be accounted for, she hurried toward the betting windows. Her betting money, the playback dough that came by wire each day, was already separated into piles of twenties, fifties, and hundreds. She used the twenties and fifties as much as her restricted time would allow, usually five and ten at a time. With the hundreds she was more cautious; they were discarded with downright stinginess.

Possibly, rather probably, much of her caution was wasted. The treasury agents had no interest in the betting; they were normally on the lookout only for wins, the cashing in of fistfuls of fifty and hundred dollar tickets. And Jasmine was not there to bet, and rarely did. Her activities were largely precautionary, not usually concerned with favorites or semi-favorites. The odds on such greyhounds pretty much took care of themselves. She dealt mainly in 'likely' runners and long-shots, and they rarely wound up in the money. When they did, she collected on them only when it seemed absolutely safe. If it didn't, she simply let the winnings go, keeping the pari-mutuel tickets as a matter of record.

To an extent, she was a free agent. She had certain general commands, but within them she was authorized and expected to use her own judgment. That didn't make things any easier for her, of course. On the contrary. It was a hard job, and she was well paid for it. And there were ways of adding to that pay.

Ways which Ethan Riley gives dirty looks upon, but which were very difficult to find out.

She strolled off toward one of the bars, her eyes acutely watchful behind the dark sunglasses. Several times she stooped quickly and picked up a discarded ticket, adding them to the ones in her purse. Losing tickets were usually thrown away. As long as they weren't torn or suspiciously threaded, she could count them as money spent.

A certain number of them, anyway. It wasn't something you could lean on too hard. She'd only gone overboard once at this meet, and that had been a mistake. Rather, she'd done it to cover a mistake.

It had happened almost a month ago, right after Michael had gone into the hospital. Perhaps that was how it had come about, she'd had her mind on her brother instead of her job. But, anyway, a real dog had come in at a hundred-and-forty for two. And she didn't have a dime down on him.

She'd been too startled and worried to sleep that night. She'd been even more disturbed the next day when the papers hinted at heavy off-track betting on the shrew. As an expensive but necessary precaution, she'd sent eighty thousand dollars of her own money back to Castries, her pretended winnings on the greyhound. And apparently that had taken the heat off of her, for she'd had no word from Ethan. But days passed before she was resting easily.

For a while, she was even carrying a handgun when she went to the bathroom.

She stood at the bar, sipping a Mount Gay Rum and cola, looking at the swarming crowd with something approaching distaste. Where did they come from? she thought dejectedly. Why did they buck a stupid racket like this? Many of them were downright scruffy. Some of them even had children with them.

Mothers with children, Men in cheap sport-shirts and baggy trousers, Grandmothers with cigarettes or roll ups, dangling from their mouths.

Gees! It was enough to turn a person's stomach.

She turned away from them, shifting sluggish from foot to foot. She was wearing a sports outfit; a simple but expensive combination of camel colored slacks, blouse, and jacket, with flat-heeled sheepskin oxfords. Everything was cool and lightweight, the most comfortable things she could put on. But nothing could make up for her hours of standing.

As the sixth and seventh races dragged by, as she moved back and forth from the betting and pay-off windows, the struggle between her growing tiredness and the never-ending need to be alert almost reached a standstill. It was hard to think of anything but sitting down, of resting for at least a few minutes. It was impossible to think about it. Need and necessity fought with one another, pulling her this way and that, tugging her forward and holding her back; adding intolerably to the weight she already carried.

There were seats in the grandstand, of course, but those were for peasants. By the time she got into the stands, she would be due at the windows. The effort of going back and forth would take more from her than it gave. As for the clubhouse, with its comfortable chairs and pleasant cocktail lounge, well, naturally, that was out. There was too much money floating around, too much heavy betting. The treasury boys loved the place.

She set down her cup of coffee, her second in the last hour and plod away toward the mutuel windows. The seventh race, the last, was coming up. It always drew some of the day's heaviest play, and the peasants were rushing to buy tickets. As Jasmine pushed her way through them, an ironic thought suddenly struck her. And despite her exhaustion, she almost laughed out loud.

Now, isn't this something? she thought. Four years getting out of the mob, and I'm right back in it. Hell, I've never even been away!

She collected a couple of bets on the seventh, disposing of the money as she hurried toward the parking lot. There was nothing in the last race that couldn't be missed. By beating it out now, before the crowd swarmed down from the stands, she could avoid the last-minute traffic jam.

Her car was parked back near the gate, in a space as near to it as a big tip would buy. A Jaguar convertible, it was a very good car and also one of the most expensive. It was very flashy. Its one distinctive feature was something that couldn't be seen. A secret trunk compartment containing eight hundred and sixty thousand dollars in cash.

As she approached the car now and saw the man standing beside it, Jasmine wondered whether she'd ever live to spend the money.

Chapter 10

Ethan Riley had curly, gray hair and a deeply tanned, lean looking face. He was a short man, five feet seven in height that is, but he had the head and chest of a six-footer. Knowing his sensitivity about his height, Jasmine was grateful for her flat-heeled shoes. That was one thing in her favor at least. But she doubted that it would count for much, judging by his expression.

He addressed her tonelessly, his lips barely moving.

'You goddamned silly-looking guzzler! Driving a goddamned circus convertible! Why don't you paint a quintain on it? Hang a couple of chains on the bumper?'

'Now, Ethan. Convertibles are quite common in Castries.'

'Convertibles are quite common in Castries,' Ethan makes fun of her, weaving his shoulders like a goody-two-shoes. 'Are they as popular as two-timing, double-crossing slut? Hah? Are they, you cunning little harlot?'

'Eth'--she looked around rapidly. 'Hadn't we better go someplace private?'

He drew back a hand as though to punch her, then gave her a shove toward the car. 'Get with it,' he said. 'The Coconut Bay. I get you alone, and I'm going to snap every bump on your pretty prime bum!'

She started the car and drove out through the gate. As they joined the stream of town-bound traffic, he started again his tight-lipped abuse.

Jasmine listened carefully, trying to decide whether Ethan was building up steam or letting it off. Probably the last, she guessed, since it had been almost two weeks since her error. Murderously angry, he probably would have taken action before this.

Most of the time she was silent, making no reply except when it was asked for or seemed urgently indicated.

'. . . told you to watch that sixth race, didn't I? And, by God, you really watched it, didn't you? I bet you stood there smiling from ear to ear clear to your ankles while the greyhound came in at a hundred-and-forty per!'

'Ethan, I--'

'How much did your friends cut you in the scheme for, heh? Or did they give you the same kind of screwing you gave me? What the hell are you, anyway, a person with compulsive sexual behavior?'

'I was down on the grumbler,' Jasmine said quietly. 'You know I was, Ethan. After all, you wouldn't have wanted me to bet it off the board.'

'You were down on it, heh? Now, I'll ask you just one question. Do you want to stick to that story, or do you want to keep your teeth?'

'I would like to keep my teeth.'

'Now, I'll ask you one more question. Do you think I got no contacts out here? You think I couldn't get a report on the play on that greyhound?'

'No, I don't think that. I'm sure you could, Ethan.'

'That moaner paid off at just the opening price. There wasn't hardly a wager on the tote board from the time the odds were posted.' He lit a cigarette, took a couple of quick angry puffs. 'What kind of crap are you handing me anyway, Jasmine? There ain't enough action to tickle the tote, but you claim a twenty five grand win! Now, how about it, huh? Are you ready to talk straight or not?'

She drew in a deep breath. Hesitated. Nodded. There was only one thing to do now, to tell the truth and hope for the best.

She did so. Ethan sat turned in the seat; studying, scrutinizing her expression throughout the recital. When she had finished, he faced back around again, sat in stolid silence for several minutes.

'So you were just dull,' he said. 'Asleep at the switch. You think I'm going to buy that?'

Jasmine nodded evenly. He'd already bought it, she said, two weeks ago; suspected the truth before he was told. 'You know you did, Ethan. If you hadn't, I'd be dead by now.'

'Maybe you will be yet, sister! Maybe you'll wish you were dead.'

'Maybe.'

'I laid out better than a hundred metres for a mugging. Just about the highest-priced piece of tail on record. I figure on getting what I paid for.'

'Then you'd better do some more figuring,' Jasmine said. 'I'm not that kind of punching bag.'

'Real sure about that, are you?'

'Positive. Give me a cigarette, please.'

He took a cigarette from his package, and threw it across the seat. She picked it up, and fling it back to him.

'Light it please, Ethan? I need both hands in this traffic.'

She heard a sound, something between a laugh and a razz, anger and admiration. Then, he lit the cigarette and placed it between her lips.

As they drove on, she could sense the looks he tinted at her, almost seeing the workings of his mind. She was a problem to him. A very special and valued employee, one whom he actually liked, had yet misjudged badly. It was unintentional, her one serious mistake in more than four years of faithful service. So there was a strong argument for forgiveness. On the other hand, he was showing unfamiliar endurance in allowing her to live, and more hardly seemed to be specified.

Clearly, there was much to be said for both sides of the discussion. Having forgiven so much, he could forgive completely. Or having forgiven so much, he needs to forgive no more.

They were almost at the hotel before he reached his decision.

'I got a lot of people working for me, Jasmine. I can't have things like this happening.'

'It never happened before, Ethan.' She fought to keep her voice level, free of any hint of begging. 'It won't happen again.'

'It happened once,' he said. 'With me, that's practically making a habit of it.'

'All right,' she said. 'You're calling the shots.'

'You got any kind of tall coat in the car? Anything you can wear to your home over your clothes?'

'No.' A dry as a dust ache came into her stomach.

He hesitated, then said it didn't matter. He'd lend her his overcoat. 'Ought to be right in style out here. Goddamnit slap dash looking women I have ever seen.'

She stopped the car at the hotel entrance, and an attendant took charge of it. Ethan handed her out to the steps, then courteously gave her his arm as they entered the building. They crossed the entrance hall, Ethan holding himself very erect, and entered the elevator.

He had a suite on the second floor. Unlocking the door, he motioned for her to go ahead of him. She did so, letting her body go hobble, preparing herself for what she knew was coming. But you could never prepare for a thing like that, not fully. The sudden thrust sent her hurtling into the room, stumbling and tripping over her own feet. And finally landing in a plunging sprawl on the floor.

As she slowly picked herself up, he locked the door, drew the shades, and entered the bathroom, emerging immediately with a large towel.

Ethan drew closer. He stopped in front of her. He moved to one side and a little behind her.

He gripped the towel with both hands. And swung.

And let the bath soaps spill harmlessly to the floor.

He motions.

She bent to pick up the bath and face soaps. And then again she was reclined. And his knees were on her back and his hand was against her head. And she was pinned, spreadeagled, against the carpet.

A couple passed in the hallway, laughing and talking. A couple from another planet. From the dining room, from another world, came the faint sound of music.

There was the click of a cigarette, roll up lighter, the smell of smoke. Then, the smell of bruised flesh as he held the wet towel against the back of her right hand. He held it with steaded firmness, just enough to keep it bruising without crushing it out.

His knees worked with expert savagery

It was a timeless world, an endless hell. There was no break out from it. There was no relief in it. She couldn't cry out. It was impossible even to wriggle. The world was at once to be lived through and insufferable. And the one possible relief was within her own small body.

And Ethan stood up, releasing her, and she got up and went into the bathroom.

She held her hand under the ice-water tap, then patted it with a towel and examined it. The bruise was ugly, but it didn't appear to be serious. None of the large veins were affected. The overcoat would cover up her stained clothes.

She left the bathroom, crossed to the lounge where Ethan was seated, but refused the drink he gave her. He took out his wallet, and extended a thick sheaf of new bills.

'Your twenty grand, Jasmine. I almost forgot.'

'Cheers, Ethan.'

'How are you making out these days, anyway? looting much from me?'

'Not much. My parents didn't raise any dunce children,' Jasmine said. 'I just clip a buck here and a buck there. It mounts up, but nobody gets hurt.'

'That's right,' Ethan Riley nodded approvingly. 'Take a little, leave a little.'

'I look at it this way,' Jasmine said, shrewdly enunciating his own philosophy. 'A person that doesn't look out for himself is too stupid to look out for anyone else. He's a liability, right, Ethan?'

'Certainly! You're a hundred percent right, Jasmine!'

'Or else he's working an angle. If he doesn't steal a little, he's stealing big.'

'Right!'

'I like that suit, Ethan. I don't know what there is about it, but somehow it makes you look so much taller.'

'Yeah?' He twinkled at her. 'You really think so? You know a lot of people have been telling me the same thing.'

Their amiable talk continued as dimness slid into the room. And Jasmine's hand ached, and the wet clothes burned and gall her flesh. She had to leave him feeling good about her. She had to make sure that the score between them was settled, and that he was actually letting her off so lightly.

They discussed several business matters she had handled for him in the city and the bars in other towns on her circuitous way to the coast. Ethan revealed that he was only in town for the day. Tomorrow he was heading back further up north.

'Another drink, Jasmine?'

'Well, just a short one. I've got to be rushing along pretty soon.'

'What's the hurry?! thought maybe we could have dinner together.'

'I'd like to, but . . .'

It was best not to stay, best to quit while she was ahead. She'd been very, very lucky apparently, but luck could run out on you.

'I've got a brother living here, Ethan. A salesman. I don't get to see him very often, so . . .'

'Well, sure, sure,' he nodded. 'How's he making out?'

'He's in the hospital. Some kind of chest trouble. I usually visit him every night.'

'Sure, naturally,' he frowned. 'Getting everything he needs? Anything I can do?'

Jasmine thanked him, shaking her head. 'He's doing well. I think he'll be getting out in a few days or so.'

'Well, you'd better run along,' Ethan said. 'The young lad's sick, he wants his sister and any close relatives by his side.'

She got the overcoat out of the closet, and belted it around her. They said good night, and she left.

A little sweat had trickled down her face, making it itch and sting, and leaving an unpleasant smell in the air. The ache in her hand grew, spread slowly up into her wrist and arm.

She hoped she hadn't soiled Ethans lounge. She'd been very lucky, considering the amount her blunder must have cost him, but a little thing like that might spoil it.

She picked up her car, and drove away from the hotel.

As she entered her house, she kicked out of her shoes, began flinging her clothes from her, leaving them in a trail behind her as she hurried toward the bathroom. She closed its door. Standing warily, she went down in front of the face basin as though it were an altar, and a great sob shook her body.

Weeping hysterically, laughing and crying, she began to spew up.

Lucky. . .

Got off easy. . .

Damn, am I lucky!_

Chapter 11

A few minutes before one in the early afternoon, Emily Casey came out of the wide door of the hospital and crossed the street to the parking lot. She'd risen unusually early that day in order to turn herself out with extra care, and the result was all that she could have hoped for. She was a stunning dream, a fragrant sultry-eyed vision of loveliness. The nurses had looked after her jealousy as she tripped down the corridor. The doctors and interns had almost drooled, their eyes lingering on the delicate shaking of her breasts and the sensual swing of her rounded little hips.

Women almost always disliked Emily. She was happy that they did, taking it as a compliment and returning their dislike. Men, of course, were invariably drawn to her, a reaction which she expected and cultivated but was emotionally cold to. Very rarely did they appeal to her. Michael Chivers was one of the rare ones who did. In her own way, she had been loyal, so faithful to him during the three years of their acquaintance.

Michael was fun, excited. Michael stirred her. Man-wise, he was the luxury which she had clutched to herself no more than four times in her life. Four men out of the ones who tried but only four who had had her body.

If she could put him to practical use, fine. She hoped and believed she could do just that. If not, she still wanted him, the sex was hot, wild, pure satisfaction, and she did not intend to have him taken from her. It wasn't, of course, that she absolutely couldn't do without him;

women who got that way over a man were strictly for the feature films. But she simply couldn't afford such a loss, it's a clear threat to her security.

When things reached the point where she couldn't hold a man, then she was finished. She might as well do a high boner out of the nearest window.

So today she had risen early, knocking herself out to be a knockout. Thinking that by arriving at the hospital at an off-hour, she could see Michael alone for a change and tease his appetite for what he had been missing. It was highly necessary, she felt. Particularly with his sister working against her, and throwing that sweet looking little nurse at him.

And today, after all the trouble she'd gone to, his damned high-and-mighty sister was there. It was almost as though Miss. Chivers had read her mind, naturally suspecting her visit to the hospital and busting her goddamned clothes to be there at the same time.

Glowing, Emily reached the parking lot. The pimply-faced attendant hastened to open the door of her car, and as she climbed into it, she rewarded him with a look at her beautiful legs.

She drove off the lot, breathing heavily, wishing that she could get Jasmine Chivers alone in a good dark alley. The more she thought about her recent visit the angrier she became.

That's what you got for trying to be nice to people! You tried to be nice to them and they made you look like a dolt!

'Please don't tell me that I can't really be Michael's sister, Miss. Emily Casey. I'm rather tired of hearing it.'

'Sorry! I didn't mean it, of course. You're about thirty, Miss. Chivers?'

'Just about, dear. Just about your own age.'

'I think I'd better leave!'

'I can give you a lift, if you like. It's only a Jaguar convertible, but it probably beats riding a bus.'

'Thanks! I have my bicycle with me.'

'Jasmine. Miss. Emily Casey drives a Honda.'

'Not really! But don't you think they're rather common, Miss. Emily? I know they're a very good car, but it seems like every overdressed hustler you see these days is driving a Honda.'

Emily's hands tightened on the wheel of the car.

She told herself that she could happily kill Miss. Chivers. She could strangle her with her bare hands.

At her apartment house, she turned the Honda over to the doorman, and went on through the lobby to the grille and cocktail lounge.

It was well into the one o'clock-hour now. Many of the tables were occupied, and waiters and waitresses in smart white tops were hurrying in and out of the kitchen with trays of delicately smelling food. One of them brought Emily an outsize menu. She studied it, hesitating over the filet mignon sandwich with side salad garnish.

She was hungry. Breakfast had taken over her usual unsweetened apple juice and creamy coffee. But she needed a drink more than she needed food: two or maybe more strong, reassuring drinks. And she could allow herself only so many calories a day.

Closing the menu, she handed it back to the waiter. 'Just a drink now, Kai,' she smiled. 'I'll eat later on.'

'Certainly, Miss. Casey. Rum, perhaps?'

'Mmm, no. Something with a little more character, I believe. A classic martini, say, Gin with an aromatic . And, Kai, no Triple Sec, please.'

'Emphatically!' The waiter wrote on his pad. "We always use Cointreau in a sidecar. Now, would you like the rim of the glass sugared or plain?'

'Plain. About an ounce and a half of bourbon to an ounce of Cointreau, and a twist of orange peel instead of lemon.'

'Right away, Miss. Casey.'

'And, . . .'

'Yes, Miss. Caesy?'

'I want that served in a martini glass. A thoroughly chilled glass, please.'

'Certainly.'

Emily watched him as he hurried away, her carefully composed features concealing an incipient snicker. Now, wasn't that something, she thought. No wonder the world was going to hell when a grown man pranced around in a fine suit, brown-nosing dames who made a big deal out of ordering a belt of booze! Where had it all started? she wondered. Where was the beginning of this detour which had sidetracked civilization into mixing drinks with one hand and stirring up bombs with the other?

She thought about it, not thinking in those words, of course. Simply feeling that the times were out of joint with themselves, and that the most emphasis was put on the least-worthwhile houndings.

What it all came down to really was everybody giving everybody else a hard time for no good reason whatsoever. And the point of it was that there seemed to be no way of getting on the right track. You couldn't be yourself anymore. If a woman ordered a straight double-shot with a beer chaser in a place like this, they'd probably throw her out. Facsimile, if she asked for a four Oz burger with raw onions.

You just couldn't dance to your own music. These days, you can't even hear it. She could no longer hear it. It was lost, the music which each person had inside himself, and which put him in step with things as they should be. Lost along with the big, fake man, the sarcastic introspective man, who had taught her how to listen for it.

Lucas Maddison. Lucas 'The retail entrepreneur' Maddison.

Her drink came, and she took a quick sip of it. Then, with a touch of torment, she half-emptied the glass. That helped. She could think of Lucas without wanting to break up.

She and The retailer owner had lived together for two years, two of the most awesome years of her life. It had been a kind of caravan holiday home living, the kind that most young people would turn up their noses at, but it was that way by choice not necessity. With Lucas, it seemed the only possible way to live.

They always traveled by ship on holiday cruises in those two years. They wore whatever they felt like wearing, usually summer wear or t-shirts for him and light blouses and shorts for her. When it was possible weather being kind, Lucas would have a small jar of Jack Daniels whiskey in a paper sack. Instead of eating at the lunch counters, they carried a huge lunch wrapped in foil paper and plastic containers. And every time the ship stopped, Lucas would make sure of buying gobs of candy and rum and cookies and everything else he could lay hands on.

They couldn't begin to eat so much themselves, naturally. Lucas gloried in plenitude, but he was a rather fussy eater and a very light drinker. The food and the booze where plentiful on the cruise ships, were to pass around, and the way he did it no one ever refused. He knew just the right thing to say to each person, a line of scripture, a quote from Socrates, a homely joke. Before they'd been sailing once again in an hour, everyone was eating and drinking and warming up to everyone else. And Lucas would be beaming on them as though they were a bunch of kids and he was a cherished father.

Women didn't hate her in those days.

Men didn't look at her the way they did now.

Friendliness, the ability to make friends, was The retail owner Mr Lucas Maddison stock in trade, of course. Something eventually to be cashed in on through small-town banks via a series of simple-seeming but puzzling maneuvers. But he insisted on regarding the payoffs as no more than a fair exchange. For minimal money, a thing useless and meaningless in itself, he traded great hopes and a new perspective on life. And nothing was ever managed so that the confusion would show through for what it was. The people were left with hope and belief.

What more could they want, anyway? What could be more important in life than having something to hope for and something to believe in?

For those magnificent two years, they lived on a caravan site farm on the coast, a sea-side sixty acres with completely modernized caravans and an outdoor privy. That was their best time together.

It was a three-hole privy, and sometimes they'd sit together in it for hours. Peering out at the occasional passersby on the wide road. Watching the seagull birds hop about in the yard. Talking quietly or reading from the pile of old newspapers and magazines that cluttered one corner of the building.

'Now, look at this, Emily,' he would say, pointing to an advertisement. 'While the price of steak has gone up fifty dollars a pound in the last decade, the price of coal has only advanced one and half per pound. It looks like the coal dealers are giving us quite a break, doesn't it?'

'Well . . .' She didn't always know how to respond to him; whether he was just making a shifty comment or telling her something.

'Or maybe they aren't either,' he'd say, 'when you bear in mind that meat is normally sold by the pound and coal by the ton.'

Now and then, she'd come up with just the right answer, like the time he'd pointed out that 'Two out of three doctors' took paracetamol, and what did she think about that, anyway?

'I'd say the third doctor was a lucky guy,' she said. 'He's the only one who doesn't have headaches.' And Lucas Maddison had been very pleased with her.

They got a lot of fun out of the advertisements. For those two years afterward, she could look at some nominally straightforward pronouncement and break into laughter.

Beware the rough zone--- Are sprouts lurking in your nooks and crannies? You, too, can learn to twirl!

Even now she laughed over them. But mockingly, with sardonic bitterness. Not as she and Lucas Maddison had laughed.

One day, when he was trying to dig down to the bottom of the magazine tack, it toppled over, uncovering a small box-like structure with a hole cut in the top. A young one's toilet.

Emily had made some comment about its being cute. But Lucas went on staring at it, the laughter dying in his eyes, his mouth loosening sickishly. Then he turned and whispered to her:

'I'll bet they do away with the youngsters. I'll bet it's buried down there under us . . .'

She was stunned, speechless. She sat staring at him, unable to move or speak, and Lucas seemed to take her silence for agreement. He went on talking, low voiced, even more forcing forward convincing than he normally was. And after a time, there was no reality but the hideousness he created, and she found herself nodding to what he said.

No, no child should be allowed to die. Yes, all children should live to see the birth of their grandchildren or as soon afterward their great grandchildren as possible. It was the kindest thing to do. It was the only way to experience the pointless torment life offers, the frustrating and senseless torture, the paradoxically evil mess which represented life on the planet Earth.

Subconsciously, she knew she was seeing him for the first time, and that the laughing, sociable Lucas was only a shadow fleeing its owner's convictions. Subconsciously, she wanted to scream that he was wrong, that there were no absolutes of any kind, and that the real man might well be fleeing the threat.

But she lacked the vocabulary for such thoughts, the mentality to string them together. They wandered about in her subconscious, unguided and unwilling, while Lucas, as always, was fully convincing. So, in the end, she had been coaxed. She agreed with everything he said.

And suddenly he started to foul-mouth her. So she was a pretender, too! A putrid hypocrite! She could do nothing for herself and nothing for anyone else because she believed in nothing.

From that day on The retail entrepernuer was on the sleigh. They jumped from the caravan park to Castries, and when he wasn't stone drunk he was shooting himself full of liquor. They had a hefty wedge of loot--rather Emily had it. Secretly, in the way of many wives although she was not legally his wife--she had been hidden and saving money for years. But the substantial sum she had cached wouldn't last two months at the rate he was going, so, as she saw it, there was only one thing to do. She took up toiling.

There was no stigma attached to it in their professional circle. In fact, it was an accepted practice for a woman to escort herself when her man was down on his back. But escorts, in itself, were customary, and only girls with 'class,' the expensively turned out dames, could pull down the big money. And Lucas Maddison was infuriated by a classy Emily Casey.

He grew bigoted in his charges that she was a plaster saint and 'apostate,' shouting down her pleas that she wished only to help him. Wildly, he declared that she was a harlot at heart, that she had always been a harlot, that she had been one when he met her.

That was not true. In her early working life, as a catwalk model and cocktail waitress, she had occasionally been on dates with men and received gifts in return. But it wasn't the same as harloting. She had liked the men involved. What she gave them on wedding parties and dinner dates, was given freely, without bargaining, as were their gifts to her.

So Lucas's false charges, insensibly made though they were, began to hurt more and more. Perhaps he didn't know what he was saying, or perhaps he did. But even the innocent blow of a young one can be painful, possibly more so than that of an adult since its victim cannot bring himself to strike back. His only recourse, when the pain becomes unbearable, is to put himself beyond the child's reach . . .

Emily's last memory of Lucas 'The retail entrepreneur' Maddison was that of a wildly weeping man in overalls, shouting 'Tart!' from the curb in front of their swank apartment house as a grinning taxi driver drove her away.

She wanted to leave the swindled money for him. Or half of it, at least. But she knew it was useless. It would either be stolen from him, or he would throw it away. He was beyond help--her help, in any event, and anything she might do would only extend the duration of his agony.

What had happened to him, she didn't know. Intentionally, she had tried to avoid knowing. But she hoped that he was dead. It was the best she could hope for the man she had loved so much.

Chapter 12

Emily took a long sip of her second bourbon cocktail. Feeling Just a little fidgety (she had a dismay of actual drunkenness), she grinned at the man who was approaching her table.

His name was Emerson, Adrian Emerson, and he was the manager of the apartment house. Dressed in striped trousers and a black broadcloth morning coat, he had rather close-set eyes and a fat, peevish looking face. His attempt to look stern, as he sat down, gave his little mouth a child-like scowl.

'Don't tell me, now,' Emily said seriously. 'You're the security of this establishment, and we had met each other on a safari cruise in the spring four years ago.'

'What? What are you talking about?' Adrian snapped. 'Now, you listen to me, Emily! I--'

'How is your rough zone?' Emily said. 'Are hidden sprouts lurking in your nooks and crannies?'

'Emily!' He leaned forward angrily, dropping his voice. 'I'm telling you for the last time, Emily. I want your bill settled now! Every last penny of it, your rent and all the other rates you've run up! You either pay it, or I'm locking you out of your apartment!'

'Now, Adrian. Don't I always pay my bills? Aren't they always settled ... one way or another?'

Adrian Emerson flushed, and looked over his shoulder. A half-pleading, half-whining note came into his voice.

'I can't do that any more, Emily. I simply can't! People staying over their leases, coming in ahead of their lease dates, paying money that I don't show on the books! I--I--'

'I understand.' Emily gave Adrian a sad, sultry look. 'You just don't like me any more.'

'No, no that's not it at all! I--'

'You don't either,' she gave a sulky expression, and stuck her lips up. 'If you did, you wouldn't act this way.'

'I told you I couldn't help it! I--I--' He saw the skulking mockery in her eyes. 'All right!' he grumbled. 'Laugh at me, but you're not making a mugger out of me any longer. You're nothing but a cheap little-- little--'

'Cheap, Adrian? Now, I didn't think I was cheap at all.'

'I'm through talking,' Adrian said firmly. 'Either you settle up by nine o'clock tonight or out you go, and I'll keep hold on to every thing you own!'

He stamped away with a kind of artful indignation.

Emily shrugged indifferently, and picked up her drink. He's a secret sufferer, she told herself. Stop getting up at night, men!

She signaled for her bill, penciled on a ten dollar tip for the waiter Kai. As he nodded gracefully, pulling back her chair, she told him that he, too, could learn to shake a leg.

'All you need is the magic step,' she said. 'It's as easy as one-two-three, or A-B-C.'

He laughed politely. Cloud-nine kidding was old stuff in a place like this. 'Like some more coffee before you leave, Miss. Emily?'

'Thank you, no,' Emily Casey smiled. 'The drinks were very good, Kai.'

She left the lounge, and passed back through the lobby. Recovering her car, she headed toward the downtown business locality.

All things considered, she had lived quite economically since her arrival in these parts of Castries. Economically, that is, insofar as her own money was concerned. Of the boodle with which she had skipped Dennery, she still had ninety thousand dollars, plus, of course, such readily negotiable items as her car, jewelry, and furs. But lately, she had had an increasingly strong hunch that her life here was drawing to a close, and that it was time to cash in wherever and whatever she could.

She hated to leave this part of the city; particularly hated the idea that it would mean giving up Michael Chivers. But it didn't necessarily have to mean that, and if it did, well, it just couldn't bc helped. Hunches were to be taken notice of. You did what you had to do.

Arriving downtown, she parked the car on a privately-operated lot. It was owned by a high class jewelry store, one which she had treated with condescension both as a buyer and seller, though largely the last. The security touched his cap and swung open the plate-glass doors for her, and one of the junior executives came forward, smiling.

'Miss. Emily Casy, how nice to see you again! Now, how can we serve you today?'

Emily told him. He nodded seriously, and led her back to a small private office. Closing the door, he seated her at the desk and sat down opposite her.

Emily took a diamond ring from her purse, and handed it to him. His eyes widened appreciatively.

'Beautiful,' he murmured, reaching for a magnifying glass. 'A wonderful piece of workmanship. Now, let's just see . . .'

Emily watched him, as he snapped on a gooseneck light, and turned the ring in his clean, strong hands. He had waited on her several times before. He wasn't handsome; almost homely, in fact. But she liked him, and she knew that he was strongly attracted to her.

He let the magnifying glass drop from his eye, shook his head with genuine concern.

'I can't understand a thing like this,' he said. 'It's something you almost never see.'

'How . . . what do you mean?' Emily frowned.

'I mean this is some of the finest adornment golden diamond pieces I've ever seen. Practically a work of art. But the stones, no. They're not diamonds, Miss. Emily Casey. Excellent replica, but still a replica.'

Emily couldn't believe him. Lucas had paid well over a thousand dollars for the ring

'But they must be diamonds! They cut glass!'

'Miss. Casey,' he smiled sarcastically, 'glass will cut glass. Practically anything will. Let me show you a positive test for diamonds.'

He handed her the microscope, and took an eyedropper from his desk. Carefully, he dropped a miniscule amount of water on the stones.

'Do you see how the water splashes over them, slides off in a sheet? With real diamonds it won't do that. It clings to the surface in tiny droplets.'

Emily nodded drearily, and took the microscope from her eye.

'Do you happen to know where it was purchased, Miss. Casey? I'm sure your money could be recovered.'

She didn't know. Quite possibly Lucas had bought it as a fake. 'It isn't worth anything to you?'

'Why, of course it is,' he said warmly. 'I can offer you--well, eighteen thousand dollars?'

'Very well. If you'll give me a check, please.'

He excused himself, and left for several minutes. He returned with the check, placed it in an envelope for her and sat down again.

'Now,' he said, 'I hope you're not too badly disappointed with us. You'll give us an opportunity to serve you again, I hope.'

Emily got caught in two minds. She glanced at the small sign on his desk. Mr. Todd. The store was named Todd's. The owner's son or a family member, perhaps?

'I should have told you, Miss. Emily Casey. With a valued customer, such as you, we'd be very happy to call at your home. It's not at all necessary for you to come to the store. If there's anything you think we might be interested in . . .'

'I have only one thing, Mr. Todd.' Emily looked at him evenly. 'Are you interested?'

'Well. I'd have to see it, of course. But--'

'You are seeing it, Mr. Todd. You're looking right at it.'

He looked puzzled, then startled. Then, his face assumed something of the same expression it had worn when he was examining the replica diamond ring.

'You know something, Miss. Emily? A bracelet like the one you sold us, we rarely run across anything like that. A fine setting and workmanship are usually indicative of precious stones. It always hurts me when I find they're not. I always hope'--he raised his eyes--'that I'm mistaken.'

Emily smiled, liking him better than ever.

'At this point,' she said, 'I think I should say oh dear.'

'Say it for both of us, Miss. Emily,' he laughed. 'This is one of those times when I almost wish I wasn't married. Almost.'

They walked to the entrance together, the lovely smartly-dressed woman and the homely, clean-looking young man. As they said good-bye, he held her hand for a moment.

'I hope everything straightens out for you, Miss. Emily. I do wish I could have helped.'

'Just stay in there and cast your sales,' Emily told him. 'You're on the right team.'

Very hungry by now, she had tea and a small potato salad at a main store. Then, she returned to her apartment house.

The manager was on the lookout for her, and he was knocking at her door almost as soon as she had closed it. Curtly, he thrust an itemized bill at her. Emily examined it, her eyebrows raising now and then.

'A lot of money, Adrian Emerson,' she murmured. 'You wouldn't have padded it a little, would you?'

'Don't you talk to me that way! You owe every damnable cent of it and you know it, and by golly you're going to pay it!'

'Maybe I could get the cash from your wife, do you suppose, Adrian? Maybe your youngsters would crack their piggy banks?'

'You leave them out of this! You go near my family, and I'll--I'll--' His voice broke into a pleading whine. 'Y-you .. you wouldn't do that, would you Emily Casey?'

Emily gave him a disgusted look. 'Oh, don't wet your pants, for God's sake! Mark the damned bill paid, and I'll get you the money.'

She turned suddenly and entered her bedroom. Opening her purse, she took out a roll of bills and dropped it on the dressing table. Then, as she undressed quickly, slipping into a sheer black negligee, her weary frown suddenly broke and she giggled.

Laughing silently, she-spread herself out on the bed.

She often broke into sudden fits of cheerfulness. Faced with some unpleasant facet of the present, she would force her mind away from it, letting it wander nomadically until it seized upon some ridiculous parallel or paradox. And then, for no apparent reason, she laughed.

Now, the laughter became briefly audible, and Adrian called to her suspiciously from the vicinity of the doorway.

'What are you up to, Emily? What are you laughing about?'

'You wouldn't understand, Adrian; just a little item from the luncheon menu. Come on in.'

119

He came in. He looked at her and gulped, then frantically pulled his gaze away.

'I want that m-money, Emily! I want it right now!'

'Well, there it is.' The negligee fell open as she waved her barefoot at the dresser. 'There's the money, and here's little Emily.'

He strode toward the dressing table. Just before he reached it, his step faltered and he turned slowly around.

'Emily, I--I--' He stared at her, gulping again, licking back the sudden saliva from the corners of his boyish mouth. And this time he could not pull his eyes away.

Emily looked down at herself, following the course of his gaze.

'The automatic clutch, Adrian,' she murmured. 'It comes with the de luxe upholstery and the highspeed curly zone.'

He made a little rush toward her. He stopped weakly, a hand held out in wretched appeal.

'P-please, Emily! Please, _please!_ I've been good to you! I've let you stay h-here month after month, and years after years . . . You will, won't you? Just--'

Emily said, nope, it couldn't be done. All clients must pay as they enter, and no free passes or rebates. 'That's a strict rule of the Intercourse Commerce Commission, Adrian. All common carriers are governed by it.'

'Please! You got to! _You j-just got to!_' Almost crying, he dropped down on his knees at the side of the bed. 'Oh, God, God, God! D-don't make me--'

'Only one choice to a customer,' Emily said firmly. 'The lady or the loot. So what's it going to be?' And then, as he suddenly flung himself at her, something held him back and walked out the room. Emily laughed hysterically at him. '

Forcing her mind away from the scenario and to Michael Chivers. Their last afternoon at the hotel. Why his sudden hemorrhage, anyway, a young guy with an apparently tough-iron chest? What had happened to bring it on? Or was it really on the level? Could it be some angle his sister was working to break them up?

She looked like an angel-player! Plenty like one! You could see that she was sharp as a tack and twice as hard--anyone could see it that knew their way around. And she was loaded with money, and...

Emily didn't want to think about her, the snubby little bitch! Anything else, but not her! She'd like to do something about her, but--

She rolled her eyes at the ceiling. What a character this guy Adrian was! What a disgusting character! He must be wearing thousand dollars worth of toilet water and hair trash, but it didn't really touch him. It was just sort of wrapped around him, like foil around a chunk of chicken burger, and when you got down under it Oops!

Emily tightened her lips once again, her cheeks bulging with repressed happiness. She tried to jerk her mind away from its source, from that patch nutty menu. But it just wouldn't go away, and again she was shivering with giggles.

'What's the matter?' gasped Adrian. 'How can you laugh at a--'

'Nothing. N-never mind, Adrian. I j-just--ah, ha, ha, ha--I'm s-sorry, but--ahh, ha, ha ha . . .'

121

dinners are special. Grilled hothouse tomato under generous slices of raw onions.

Chapter 13

Jasmine Chivers's house was on the top of a short hill Sunset Strip buildings a few streets west of the city limits of Castries coast line. Fully furnished, it consisted of five unsuited bedrooms, communal bath, powder room, kitchen, dining room, two sitting rooms and den. The den was on the rear or south side of the building, and a hospital bed had been put into it for Michael. He lay on it today, in cream-colored pajamas and bathrobe, his head cranked up so that he could look out over unlimited miles of sea huts, ocean, and beach towns.

He felt lazy and comfortable. He felt on edge and culpable. This was the ending of his second week out of the hospital. He was fully recovered, and there was no well founded excuse for his remaining here. And yet he loitered on. Jasmine wanted him to. The doctors passively encouraged him to, seeing little to be gained by his strung out convalescence but a broad margin of safety in it.

The ruptured vessels of his shoulder area could open up again, under just the right circumstances. They could be re-ruptured. Thus, if he wished to remain completely slothful for a couple more weeks and beyond reach of the smallest risk, it was quite agreeable with the doctors.

Aside from Jasmine and the matter of his health, Michael had another reason for staying on. A guilty reason, and one he tried not to admit to. She, Layla Ellis, was in the kitchen now, cleaning up their dinner dishes and doubtless preparing a tasty dessert for them. He didn't want any himself, he had gained almost ten pounds in the past two weeks, but he knew that she did. And not for the world would he have encroached on.

Layla was very dainty about her eating, as she was about everything. But he had never seen anyone who could put away so much food so quickly.

He wondered about that, her unquenchable appetite, when he was not wondering about her in a different way. Most women he knew seemed to hardly eat anything. Emily, for example . . .

Emily . . .

He twisted uneasily as he recalled her visit earlier on today. He had told her yesterday in a hushed telephone conversation that Jasmine was leaving the house early today, and suggested that she drop by. So she had come, pulling up startled when she saw Layla, then giving him a quick, questioning look.

Layla sat down in the sitting room with them. She apparently felt that it was only polite to do so, and she tried to make conversation about the news in the media and the usual routine topics. When, after what was probably the longest twenty five minutes on record, she had finally excused herself and gone into the kitchen, Emily turned on him, secretly.

'I tried to send her out,' Michael said helplessly. 'I told her to take off for a few hours.'

'Tried to? If it were me, you'd just say to beat it.'

'I'm sorry,' he said. 'I wanted to be alone as much as you did.'

He glanced quickly over his shoulder, then went down beside her chair and took her into his arms. She put forward a kiss, but there was no response to it. He kissed her again, letting his hands rove over her body, probing the soft, sweet-scented curves. After weeks of enforced continence, and the constant temptation which Layla represented, he had never wanted Emily as much as he did at that moment. But suddenly she had pulled away from him.

'Just how much longer do you plan on staying here, Michael?' she asked. 'When are you moving back to the Park Royal holiday apartment?'

'Well. I don't know exactly. Pretty soon, I suppose.'

'You're not in much of a hurry, are you? You like it here.'

Michael said awkwardly that he had no complaints. He was being well taken care of, much better than he could be at the Park Royal and his older sister Jasmine was yearning to have him stay.

'Woohoo, I'll bet she is, and I'll bet you're darned well taken care of, too!'

'What do you mean?'

'Are you kidding? I've seen the way you looked at that cute little numbskull of a nurse! Either you're losing your grip, or you think she's too good to topple over. She is, but I'm not!'

'Oh, for crying out loud . . .' He reddened. 'Look, I'm sorry about today. If there was any way I could get rid of her without hurting her feelings . . .'

'Naturally, you couldn't do that. Oh, no!'

'Let's just say that I wouldn't do it then,' he said, tired of making or expressing regrets.

'Well, forget it.' She picked up her gloves, and stood up. 'If it suits you, it suits me.'

He followed her out into the hallway, trying to smooth over the fault without unbending too far. Liking her, desiring her more than he ever had, yet cautious as always of any tightening of her hold upon him.

'I'll be out of here any day now,' he asserted himself to her. 'I'm probably a hell of a lot more concerned than you are.'

'Well . . .' She smiled hesitantly, the sparkling eyes searching his face. 'I'm not so sure of that.'

'You'll see. Maybe we can go to the cinema this weekend.'

'Just maybe?'

'I'm practically sure of it,' he said. 'I'll give you a ring, hmm?'

So he had got things straightened out, for a time, at least, and after a trend. But he had gotten nothing in return, nothing but the status circumstances, and unsatisfied desire turned inside him relentlessly. Something was going to have to give, he told himself. With Emily's presence still lingering with him, with Layla so readily accessible

Layla. He wondered just what he should do about her anyway. Or whether he should do anything about her. She looked completely virginal, and if she was, that was that. She'd remain that way, as far as he was concerned. But looks could be deceptive; and sometimes, when she consented to a kiss and she clung to him for a moment, well, he wasn't so sure about her status. Was, in fact, almost positive that he had judged it wrongly.

And in that case, of course . . .

She came in from the kitchen, bearing two cream topped dessert glasses. He accepted one of them, and she sat down with the other. Smiling, he watched as Layla dipped into it, wanting to sweep her up in his arms and give her a hearty squeeze.

'Good?' he said.

'Delicious!' she exclaimed enthusiastically. Then, looking up at him, jabbing with self-consciousness. 'All the time here, I am eating! You think I am such a glutton, yes?'

Michael laughed. 'If they made gobbler like you, I'd start raising them. How about eating mine, too?'

'But it is yours. Extras I could not possibly eat!'

'Sure you can,' he said, swinging his legs off the bed. 'Will you come into the bedroom when you're through?'

'I will come now. You want your Swedish massage, yes?'

'No, no,' he said quickly. 'There's no hurry. Finish your dessert first.'

He crossed the deeply carpeted living room and entered the bedroom. Entering the bedroom, he paused for a long moment, almost deciding to stop now while he could. Then, swiftly, before he could change his mind, he flung off the robe and his pajama top and stretched out on the bed.

Layla came in a few minutes later. She started to get the bio-oil bottle from the bathroom, and he held out his hand to her.

'Come here, Layla. I want to ask you something.'

She nodded, and sat down on the edge of the bed. He drew her closer, bringing her face down to his; and, then, as their lips met, he began to draw her susceptible.

Nervously, her body suddenly stiffening, she tried to pull away. 'Oh, no! Please, Michael. I--I--'

'It's fine, okay. I want to ask you something, Layla. Will you tell me the truth?'

'Well'--she tried to muster a smile. 'It's very significant to you? Or perhaps you are teasing me again, yes?'

'It's very important to me,' he said. 'Are you a virgin, Layla?'

The smile washed unexpectedly from her face, and for a moment it was something completely blank. Then, a trace of color came back into it and her eyes fell, and almost undetectable she shook her head.

'No, I am not a virgin.'

'You're not?' He was more or less disappointed.

'I am not. Not by many times.' Under its surface firmness, her voice shook slightly. 'And now you will not like me any more.'

'Not like you? Why, of course, I do. I like you more than ever!'

'But--' She smiled tremulously and began to glow with a kind of joyous lack of belief. 'You really mean it? You would not tease about such an important thing?'

'What's so important about it? Now, come on, sugar plum!'

Laughing joyously, she allowed him to pull her down against him; hugged him with giggling wonderment. Oh, my, she said. She was so happy. And then, with no real resistance, bubbling with the happiness, he had given her, 'But--shouldn't we wait, Michael? You would not like me better?'

'I couldn't like you any better!' He tugged impatiently at her blue uniform. 'How do you get this damned thing--?'

'But there is something else you must know. You have a right to know. I--I cannot have babies, Michael. Never.'

That stopped him, made him hesitate, but only for a second. She had an awkward way of phrasing things, twisting them around retropective and putting the emphasis in the wrong places. So she couldn't have toddlers and that was all to the good, but he would have taken care of that, anyway.

'Who cares?' he said, almost groaning in his hunger for her. 'It's fine and it's more than fine if you're not a virgin. Now, can't you stop talking, for God's sake, and--'

'Yes! Oh, yes, Michael!' She clung to him in wondrous surrender, guiding his fumbling hands. 'Also, I want to. And it is your right . . .'

The uniform fell away from her; the panty was peeled off slowly. The innate modesty, the fears, the past. In the drapedrawn dimness of the room, she was reborn, and there was no past but only a future.

The purplish brand still lingered on her outflung arm, but now it was purely a childhood scar; time dulled, shrunken by growth. It didn't matter. What it memorialized didn't matter--the neuter, the loss of virginity--for he had said it didn't. So the thing itself was without meaning: the indelible imprint of the asylum concentration camp.

Michael's eyes just kept staring at Layla. She is always splendidly looking in the glorious beauties of her body, and in temperament hot as the most erotic of their sex could desire. Even in his ignorance he have felt the wonderful power of bestowing lustful ecstatic pleasure she possesses, and now knows how, in the energy of her passion, she allowed her lust to betray her into the use of grossly naughty expressions, but which, as they have enlightened him when best prepared to receive such knowledge, is rather fortunate than otherwise.

His fingers sweep round, to pass between her thighs, was brave and graceful. In the middle was a well defined semi-circular shape, from whence the beautifully lips of hers commenced, which in her position lay to some degree open. You could just see where the clitoris lay cozy.

On these occasions her eyes sparkled in a curious manner, and her breathing moved slowly. After a while, her hand left Michael's arm and rested on his opposite shoulder, in a half hug, which became warmer and warmer, their conversation became more affectionate. Michael was pleased in his congratulations that his dearest had found such a charming master; and here she halted, and turned half in front of him and, stooping slightly, she sought a kiss of caring affection. Michael threw his arms around her neck, and their lips met in a long and loving kiss, very warm on Layla's side, but a simple though affectionate kiss on Michael's.

Here he again raised his lips for a squeeze, which was given with even more than the previous warmth. Her arm had fallen to his waist, and she pressed him with passion to her bosom, which he could feel was on the spur of the moment, compact, and even hard. Michael had great difficulty in keeping his unruly manhood down, that she might think he took her warm cuddles as nothing more than affectionate friendship. Michael succeeded, however, and this, of course, more than ever convinced Layla of his entire innocence of sensual desires

Michael smiled at Layla's reference to the size of his manhood, and knowing that her curiosity must be creating in her a desire to hold it, he told her it was perfectly grown for her.

Her eyes glistened, her face flushed, and she smiled most graciously on Michael. The two appeared very happy.

Layla looked so lovely in the dim light, that Michael withdrew his finger from her honeypot, he was stimulated to ask her to let him see her perfectly naked in all her glorious beauty of form with the lights brightened. She thrill him at once; but laughingly, pulled him towards her, and said;

'I, too, must have the pleasure not only of viewing your rosy youthful charms, but of embracing your dear form unchained of all the extravagance.'

They grip each other in a most enrapturing embrace, and then Michael's lovely and engaging Layla permits him to turn her in every direction so as to see, admire, and devour every charm of her exquisitely formed body. Oh my gosh! She was indeed beautiful. They caressed each other with such reciprocal satisfaction that nature soon drove them to a closer and more active union of the bodies.

 To Michael's young eyes she was a perfect goddess of beauty. Up to the present time, he can remember nothing that, as a whole surpassed her, although he have met women with points perfectly beautiful, some carry their goddess in the bosom, some in the hands, face, some in the mount of Venus and bottom together, and some in legs and thighs; but Layla was such a divine being, without having the appearance of it when dressed, was, when lay bare, perfect in all her parts as well as beautiful in face, caressing and shapely by nature, and conferring herself, with the most enchanting graces to instruct Michael in all the mysteries of love, and let him say, of desire also. Never will he forget the luxury of that squeeze.

'Layla did you know. Your entire body, Michael declared, is quite unique. Whenever you stick out your knockers when excited as far as the nipples would swell, and how, I want to play the Tiger on your belly, I believe that it will actually give you great pleasure, as indeed it gave me. I want to examine, and admire it beyond measure.'

Oh! could Layla paint Michael's figure as she sees it now, still present to her transported fascination! a whole length of an all perfect manly beauty in full sight. Think of a face without a failing, glowing with all the opening bloom and lush freshness of an age, in which beauty is of either sex, and which the first down over his upper lip scarce began to distinguish.

The parting of the double ruby mouth of Michael lips seemed to exhale an air sweeter and purer than what it drew in: oh! Whatever ferocity did it did not cost Layla to hold back the so enticing kiss!

Then a neck wonderfully turned, critical behind and on the sides with curly hair, playing freely in natural ringlets, connected his head to a body of the most perfect form, and of the most vigorous structure, in which all the strength of manhood was hidden, and softened to appearance by the elegance of his complexion, the smoothness of his skin, and the plumpness of his flesh.

Whilst Layla kept on observing, she notice the conformity of his limbs, that exactness of shape, in the fall of it towards the flank, where the waist ends and the rounding swell of the hips commences; where the skin, velvety, smooth, and dazzling, burnishes on; the span firm, plump, ripe flesh, that groove and ran into dimples at the least pressure, or that the touch could not rest upon, but slid over on the surface of the most polished body.

His thighs, were finely formed, and with a flamboyant glossy roundness, gradually building away to the knees, seemed stanchion worthy to support that beauteous frame at the bottom of which she could not, without some remains of alarm, some tender emotions too, fix her eyes on that broad manhood, which had, been longing to, with such savagery broke into, rip, and almost ruined those soft, tender parts of hers, that had not yet done smarting with the effects of its rage; but behold it now! peak immoral, reclining its mantle manhood head over one of his thighs, quiet, docile, and to all appearances incapable of the naughtiness and cruelty it had committed.   Then the magnificent growth of the hair, in short and soft curls round its roots, its burnt sienna, branched veins, the agile mellowness of the rod, as it lay contracted, rolled and shrunk up into a squat broadness, idle, and shored up from between his thighs, by its globular addition, that wondrous treasure bag of the universe delights, which roister round, and pursed up in the only wrinkles that are known to please, perfected the prospect, and completely formed the most interesting moving picture in the universe, and surely infinitely superior to those nudities furnished by the sculptor, statues, or any art, which are purchased at monumental prices; whilst the sight of them in actual life is scarce supremely experienced by any but the few whom nature has furnished with a flame of curiosity warmly pointed by a truth of judgment to the jumble, the originals of beauty, of nature's unmatched composition, above all the replicas of craft.

As to character, the even amiability of it made him seem born for domestic happiness: tender, naturally civil, and kind hearted; it could never be his culpability, if ever drums, or animosities irritate a calm he was so competent in every way to maintain or restore. Without those great or shining qualities that comprise a genius, or are apt to make a noise in the world, he had all those respectful ones that compose the softer social merit: plain common sense, set off with every grace of directness and good nature, made him, if not admired, what is much happier: in all cases beloved and approve of. But, as nothing but the beauties of his person had at first attracted Layla's regard and secured her passion, neither was she then an officiate of the internal caliber, which she had afterwards full motive to uncover, and which, perhaps, in that season of reeling and cheeriness, would have touched her heart a bit, had it been fixed in a person less the delight of her eyes, and icon of her senses.

Layla's homeland accent, and the verdant of her stride, style, and etiquette began now sensibly to wear off: so quick was her observation, and so fruitful her desire of growing every minute worthier of his heart. he managed so, at least, as to give her the satisfaction of believing it impossible for him to be more poignant, more true, more faithful than he was.

Michael lay then all trained and passive as Layla could wish, whilst her freedom raised no other emotion but those of a wild, and, till then, unfelt pleasure. Every part of Layla was open and exposed to the licentious courses of Michael's hands, which, like a bedazzling fire, ran over her entire body, and warmed all coldness as they went.

Some lascivious touches from Michael had lighted up a new fire that wantoned through all Layla's veins, but fixed with violence in that center appointed them by nature, where Mihael's fingers were now busied in feeling, squeezing, compressing the lips, then opening her honeypot again, with a finger between, till an 'Oh!' expressed him pleasuring her, where the narrowness of the unbroken passage refused it entrance to any depth.

Layla' heated and alarmed senses were in a rumpus that robbed her of all liberty of thought; tears of pleasure gushed from her eyes, and somewhat assuaged the fire that raged all over her.

Michael's sight must be feasted as his touch. He must devour with his eyes this springing bosom. Oh he longs to kiss her beautiful breast more and more. Michael has not seen it enough. Oh he wanted to kiss and lick them once more. 'What firm, smooth, beautiful flesh is here! How delicately shaped! Then this delicious honeypot! Oh! let me view the small, dear, tender cleft! This is too much, I cannot bear it! I must! I must!' Michael cried out. Here he took his fingers, and in a transport carried it to her honeypot. But what a difference in the state of the same thing!. The cavity to which he guided his fingers readily

135

received it; and as soon as Layla felt it within her, she moved herself to and fro, with so rapid a friction, that he presently withdrew it, wet and juicy, when instantly Layla grew more composed, after four or five more sighs, and heart-fetched Oh's! and giving Layla a kiss that seemed to exhale her soul through her lips. What pleasure she had found, Michael could not tell; but this he knew, that the first sparks of kindling nature, the first ideas of pollution, were caught by Michael that evening; and that the acquaintance and communication with the heat of their sexual encounter, is often as fatal to innocence as all the seductions of the other.

At twenty two years of age; Michael's hips and thighs were well projected. His body was finely formed, and of a most vigorous make, square shouldered, and broad chested: For, besides all the perfections of manly beauty which were assembled in his form, he had an air of neatness and coolness, certain smartness in the shape and port of his head, that yet more distinguished him; his eyes were sprightly and full of meaning; his looks had in them something at once seen, sweet and commanding; his skin tone out-bloomed the lovely colored rose, whilst its inimitable tender vivid glow clearly saved it from the reproach of wanting life, of raw and dough-like, which is commonly made of those so extremely fair as he was.

Then his grand motions, which seemed to rise out of a spread of short hair that spread from the root all over his thighs, his hammer or dick stood stiff and upright, but of a size to fluster Layla, it was ten and a half inches long the helmet of it alone filled the utmost capacity of her grasp. By harmony for the small tender honeypot which was the object of its fury, and which now lay exposed to Michael's clairest view. Her thighs were spread out to their utmost extension, and between them the mark of the sex, the pink serene cleft of flesh, the lips smooth inwards, showed a minute scarlet line in sweet diminutive.

By now Michael had changed her posture from lying breadth to another position on the bed: but Layla's thighs were still spread, and the mark lay fair for him, who now displayed a view of that fierce erect prick of his, which threatened no less than splitting the tender Layla who lay smiling at the uplifted stroke, nor seemed to reject it. He looked upon his manhood himself with some pleasure, and guiding it with his hand to the inviting; slit, drew aside the lips, and lodged it after several slow hard thrusts, about half way; but his ten and a half inches long pecker got stuck, because of its growing swelling, and thickness: Michael draws it again, and poured some oil in his hands, and rubbed it gently over his pecker and re-enters, and with a better ease, sheathed it now up to the hilt, at which Layla gave a deep sigh, which was quite another tone than one of pain; he rams, she heaves, at first gently, and in a regular rise and fall; but presently the transport began to be too violent to observe any order or measure; their motions were too rapid, their kisses too fierce' and fervent for nature to support such fury long: both seemed to be in a battle: their eyes darted fires: 'Oh! oh! I can't bear it. It is too much. I am going,' were Layla's expressions of ecstasy: Michael's joys were more silent: but soon broken murmurs, sighs heart-fetched, and at length a dispatching thrust, as if he would have forced himself up her body. Michael decided to lie down on his back, and gently pull down Layla upon

137

him, who giving way to his humor, mounted, and with her hands conducted her blind favorite to the right place; and following her impulse, ran directly upon the flaming point of this manhood of pleasure, which she bolster up herself upon, up pierced, and affixed to the extremest hair breadth of it: thus Layla sat on Michael a few instants, enjoying and relishing her situation, whilst he toyed with her delicious breasts. Sometimes she would stoop to meet his kiss: but presently the sting of pleasure spurred them up to more savage action; then began the storm of heaves, which, from the undermost combatant, were thrust at the same time, Michael crossing his hands over Layla, and drawing her home to him with a sweet violence: the inverted strokes of anchor over rod soon brought on the critical period.

Speeding up then to give Layla the benefit of it, Michael turn her down on the bed; but such was the refreshed soreness of those part, on Layla leaning so hard on them, as became her to compass the admission of that astounding helmet of his prick, that she could hardly bear it. Layla got up then, and tried, by leaning forwards, and turning the hips on Michael, to let him drive at different angles: but here it was likewise difficult to stand Michael's bearing so fiercely against her, in his ruffles and attempts to enter that way, whilst his stomach pounded directly against the recent sore.

Both intolerably heated: both in a fury; but pleasure is ever inventive for its own ends: and placing a two broad couch-cushion on the floor, oversets Layla gently on it; and handles her only at the waist. Layla brought her legs around Michael's neck; so that her head was kept from the floor only by her hands and the cushions: therefore she stood on her head and hands, supported by Michael in such manner, that whilst her thighs clasp around him, so as to expose to his sight all her lovely figure, including the theater of Michael's pleasure, the center of her honeypot fairly bearded the object of its rage, that now stood in fine condition to give her satisfaction.

But as this posture was certainly not the easiest, and their imaginations, wound up to the height, could suffer no delay, Michael first, with the utmost eagerness and effort, just rammed his broad helmet of his dick; and still befriended by the fury with which he had made that impression, he soon stuffed in the rest; when now, with a pursuit of thrusts, fiercely urged, he absolutely overpowered and absorbed all sense of pain and uneasiness, whether from her bruises, or the oversize of his long, broad manhood, in an infinitely predominant pleasure; when now all Layla's whole spirits of life and sensation rushing, impetuously to the g-spot, where the prize of pleasure was hotly in dispute and clustering to a point there.

Romped up with a craving of so greedy appetite, to meet and favor the hard thrust of insertion, that the fierce activity on both sides effected it with such pain of distention, that Layla cried out violently, that she was hurt beyond bearing. But it was too late: the commotion was up, and force was on her to give way to it; for now the fat manhood, strongly worked upon by the sensual passion, felt so manfully his advantages and superiority, felt withal the sting of pleasure so excruciating, that maddening with it, his joys began to assume a character of furiousness,

Goring then all before him, and mad and wild like an galvanized steer, Michael work up the tender furrow all insensible to Layla's complaints; nothing can stop, nothing can keep out a fury like his: with which, having once got its helmet in, its blind rampage soon made way for the rest, piercing, jamming, and breaking open all barriers.

And before long now, by cleft of an enraged enforcement, the stiff manhood, driven like a whirlwind, made all smoke again, and wedging its way up, to the utmost extremity, left her, in point of penetration, nothing to fear or to desire: and now, Layla lay, pleased to the heart, pleased to her utmost capacity of being so, with every fiber in her inner parts, stretched almost to breaking, on a rack of joy, whilst the manhood of all this over-fullness searched her senses with its sweet excess, till the pleasure gained upon her so, its point stung her so home, that catching at length the rage from her furious driver Michael, and sharing the riot of his wild rapture, she went wholly out of her mind into that favorite part of her body, the whole intenseness of which was so alarmingly filled: there alone she existed, all lost in those delirious transports, those ecstasies of the senses, which her blinking eyes, the brightened crimson of her lips and cheeks, and sighs of pleasure deeply fetched, so pitifully showed.

Michael made her feel with a vengeance his tempestuous manhood he battered with; their active loins quivered again with the violence of their conflict, till the surge of pleasure, foaming and raging to a height, drew down the ivory shower that was, to allay this tornado.

Then at first Michael shed those tears of joy that attend its last moments, not without an agony of delight, and even almost a roar of rapture, as the gush escaped him; so sensibly too for Layla, that she kept him faithful company, going off, in consent, with the old symptoms: a delicious delirium, a tremendous convulsive shudder, and the critical dying: Oh Michael! And now, on his getting off she lay pleasure-drenched, and regorging its essential delights; and gasping for breath, without other sensation of life than in those exquisite vibrations that trembled still on the strings of delight; which had been too intensively touched, and which nature had so ravishingly stirred with, for the senses to be quickly at peace from. as he stood with his label of manhood, now lank, unstiffened, becalmed, and flapping against his thighs, down which it reached half way. They kissed and cuddled for sometime, before heading to the bathroom for a much needed shower. And then off to bed for a much needed sleep.

It was a cool and lovely morning. Layla was sitting up in the bed, she was wearing only a t-shirt and panties her nurse uniform were all tossed, or rolled off, by the unquietness of their motions, from the erotic passions on the lovely hours before; nor could she refuse herself a pleasure that solicited her so temptingly, as this fair occasion of feasting her sight with all those treasures of Michael's beauty she had enjoyed, and which lay now almost entirely naked, his underwear being fettered up in a perfect lock, which the warmth of the season and room made her easy about the consequence of. She hung over him besotted indeed! and guzzled all his naked charms with her seductive two eyes, when she could have wished them at least a thousand for the fuller enjoyment of the gaze.

Upon awakening Michael watches Layla next to the dressing table busy typing away on her laptop and writing on a notebook. Michael roused out of the bed, tasted her soft lips and the kissing of her delicious breasts, so that she felt joys of which she would never tire. On this occasion though, Layla smacked Michael's bare bottom and sent him off to the bathroom, so that they both might get ready for some snacks, for which their appetites were already craving. Michael slipped on a dressing-gown, went into the bathroom, then to the kitchen to make Layla a hearty sandwich so that by the time she had finished writing, showered and dressed, it would be a surprise for her. Layla decided to write a journal diary of her first evening with Michael, love session detailing;

Hi Michael. How can I ever sufficiently thank my darling for his appetizing love? I've this little journal book to detail our sensual encounters. I will keep it in my study room, and renew the pleasure of its perusal at every spare moment. Oh! with such a pleasant energy of description. Never in my life have I enjoyed such an exquisite description of those dear erotic encounters. How delighted I am at your good fortune in meeting with such a prodigy of a young lad as that dear Michael. Why, he has every quality of a man, united to the charm of extreme youth. What a grandiose man he will become, the very perfection of a lover, and already possessing so lustful desires and lascivious lubricity. Oh my gosh! How I enjoyed his broad tough manhood. What luck for him too, to have fallen into the hands of such

142

a flavorsome nurse as me. Am I not myself his pupil, and were he not my own very enjoyable instructer in all that one of our sex could teach each other.

In fact, my dear Michael, I may say it was the first sexual encounter that thoroughly made me realize, or rather our, excitements of the act. We arranged the line of behavior necessary to be followed so as to agree with us. In a short time we had again a very enjoyable sex position, with outstretched legs, on a bed, on the floor, you got me to mount on top of you, and sink down on your hard upstanding manhood. I have tried this position once before, but it does not equal our sex. One has so much better a spring from one's feet than from one's knees, besides, the man is brought more face to face, and there is more space for joint enclasps; but both ways have their allure.

I must tell you, your compact collector's item box, I did; you know how powerfully you Michael is hung, and loving you as I do, it is impossible to undergo your powerful and libidinous cuddles without feeling all one's erotic passions stirred up within me, but even while in your possession, my dear young lover, I thought of your young charms, and the untamed delights we had enjoyed together this first evening we made love. that I was thinking and vitalizing myself to wild convulsions of voluptuous movements, while you were making merry in all the lustfulness of passions, and sexing me to my heart's satisfactions.

I'll never forget how our rounds would end in rapturous joys, beyond the power of illustration, and how you swagger along as proud as a peacock, and thought no small Tiger of yourself.

Michael turned towards Layla whom he noticed was busy writing away with a notebook. It was evident her dreams or visualizing had brought back some loved and happy man and no doubt the fact of him being in possession, had made her believe in the reality of her happy thoughts.

Then Layla's eye caught Michael's face....

Oh! my darling Michael, it is you! I have been dreaming of being far away, and, I suppose, the fact of your dear manhood pounding within me made me think of heaven. Well, the fantasies had its pleasures.'

Layla decided to share the events of her journal with Michael, of her romantic story.

Michael could not help throwing himself into Layla's arms for a loving embrace. Layla could hardly voice her blessing, and Michael saw the tears flowing down her honored cheeks as she waved her face cloth but like all things the diary had to end there for now. And they reached for bed and sobbed themselves in each other arms

.

Chapter 14

Layla came out of the bathroom, modestly wearing her panties now; still flushed and warm and glowing. Primly protective, she drew up the sheet and tucked it over Michael's chest. 'I must take care of you,' she said. 'Now, more than ever, you are most important to me.'

Michael grinned at her lazily. She was sweet, a lot of women, he thought. And about the most honest one he'd ever met. If she hadn't told him that she can't have toddlers. . .

'You are all right, Michael? You do not hurt any place?'

'I never felt better in my life,' he laughed. 'Not that I haven't been feeling okay.'

'That is good. It would be terrible if I had hurt you.'

He repeated that he was feeling well; she was just what he'd needed. She said seriously that she also had needed him, and hc laughed again, winking at her.

'I believe you, babes. How long has it been, anyway, before me, or shouldn't I ask?'

'How long?' She moaned a bit, her head tilted in bewilderment. Then, 'Oh,' she said. 'Well, it--it was--'

'Never mind,' he said quickly. 'Forget it.'

'It was there.' She extended the inking arm. 'There also I was made barren.'

'There?' he frowned. 'I don't ... What's that, anyway?'

She explained dreamily, her smile fixing; the angled up angel eyes looking at him and through him toward something far, beyond.

Seemingly, she was speaking of the abstract, a sad and flimsy statement scarcely worthy of public performance. Seemingly, she was reading from a fairy tale, a thing so filled with horrors that they clung stagnating to one another; never advancing the plot or theme, physically motionless, merely terror stacked upon terror until they sagged slowly downward, drawing the listener with them.

'Yes, yes, that is right.' She smiled at him as though at 'an old before one's years youngster.'. 'Yes, I was very young, eight or nine, I think. That was the reason, you see: to discover the earliest possible age at which a female might develop. It can be very early in life, I think. But an average minimum age was being sought. With my parents and grandparents, it was the other way; I mean, how old could the female be. My grandmother died shortly after the beginning of the experiment, but my mother . . .'

Michael wanted to spew up. He wanted to hold her, to cuddle her. Standing apart from himself, as she was standing from herself, he was furious with her experience. Subjectively, his thoughts were not a distant alignment with the current popular philosophizing. The things you heard and read and saw everywhere. The devoted mourning of sin; the joyous absolution of the sinners; the uncomfortable frowns and glances disdainfully at those who recalled their misdeeds. After all, the one-time acquaintances, poor fellows, were now our friends and it was in bad taste to show torture on television.

'Well, now,' Michael muttered, 'I don't want to put you in the wrong. I like you; I think the world of you, Layla. That's why I asked you what I did, told you it was important to me. I can see now how you might have taken it the wrong way, and I wish to the divine being there was something I could do to square things up. But--'

But why did she keep looking at him that way, smiling that totally vacant smile; waiting for him to fill the vacuum with life? He had said he was sorry, apologized for something that was beyond his control. But still she sat there waiting. Did she really expect him to give up his life, the only way of life acceptable to him, purely to correct a mistake? Well, she had no right to do so! Even if he could give what she had expected and apparently still desired, he could not do it.

She was a nice girl, and it wouldn't be fair to her.

'Now, I'll tell you what,' he said, smiling flatteringly. "We can't change what's already happened, Okay? We'll just make a brand new start?'

She looked at him mutely.

'Fine,' Michael said swiftly. 'That's my sweet girl.

Returning to the den, Michael flopped back down on the hospital bed, stared out unseeing at the panorama to the west; still seeing the nurse in the bedroom. He'd put things very badly, he guessed. His usual talkativeness had failed him, just when he needed it most, and he'd sounded peevish and small-time.

What had happened to him? he wondered. What had gone wrong with his pitch?

It had been an honest mistake. She'd suffered no actual loss because of it. Why couldn't he make her understand that? Why, when he could so easily pull a real swindle without a kickback?

You can't cheat an honest person, he thought. And was unreasonably irritated by the thought.

He heard her approaching, the starchy rustle of her uniform. Working up a smile, he sat up and turned around.

She was wearing her coat, a long gray garment. She was carrying her small nurse's kit.

'I am leaving now,' she said. 'Is there anything you want before I go?'

'Leaving! But-- Oh, now, look,' he said winningly. 'You can't do that, you know. It's not professional. A nurse can't walk out on a patient.'

'You do not need a nurse. We both know it. At any rate, I have ceased to be a nurse to you.'

'But--but, damnit, Layla--'

She turned away from him, started for the door. He looked after her helplessly for a moment, then caught up with her and pulled her around facing him.

'Now, I'm not going to let you do this,' he said. 'There's no reason to. You need the job, and my sister and I both want you to have it. Why--'

'Let me go, please.' She pulled away from him, again moving toward the door.

Hastily, he placed himself in front of her. 'Don't,' he begged. 'If you're angry at me, okay; maybe you think you've got a right to be. But my sister's involved here. What will she think, I mean, what will I tell her when she comes home and finds you're--'

He trails off, reddening, realizing that he had sounded fearful of Jasmine. A ghost of a smile touched Layla's lips.

'Your sister will be disappointed,' she said, 'but not surprised, I think. I thought your sister did not understand you, but now I know that she does.'

Michael looked away from her. He said curtly that that wasn't what he meant at all. 'You've got some money coming to you, your wages. If you'll tell me how much . . .'

'Nothing. Your sister paid me last night.'

'All right, then, but there's still today.'

'For today, nothing. I gave nothing of value,' she said.

Michael let out an angry burst. 'Stop acting like a little kid, will you? You've got some money coming to you, and, by God, you're going to take it!' He grabbed the wallet from his robe pocket, jerked out its bank notes and extended it toward her. 'Now, how much? What do I owe you for today?'

She looked down at the money. Carefully, shuffling through it with a finger, she selected the banknotes and held them up.

'Thank you. It is really too much.'

She turned, crossed the carpet to the door and went out.

Michael raised his hands helplessly, and let them drop to his sides. That was that. He wasn't a happy bunny. He walked to the kitchen, warmed up some coffee and drank it, standing up. Rinsing out his cup, he glanced at the clock above the cooker.

Jasmine would be home in a few hours. There was something he must do before she got here. It wouldn't make this Layla thing all right with her, and it would mean tipping his hand, but it had to be done. For his own sake.

Dressing and going down to the main road, he was just a little shaky. But not because there was anything wrong with him,only from his long headache from thinking too hard. By the time he had gotten a taxi and reached his hotel, he felt as strong as he ever had.

He was a little embarrassed by his reception at the Park Royal. Of course, he'd always worked to make himself likable; that was an essential part of his front. But he was still warmed and just about discomfited at the way he was welcomed home (_home!_) by Mr Harper and the owner's work staff. He was glad that he didn't have to fool them; leave them up the creek, defenceless, where people who liked him were generally left.

Flustered, he accepted their congratulations on his recovery, reassured them as to the present state of his health. He agreed with Mr. Harper, that sickness came to all men, always hindrance and unexpectedly, and that that was how the permanent waved.

At last, he escaped to his room.

He took fourteen thousand dollars from one of the clown pictures. Then, having carefully replaced the picture on the wall, he left the Park Royal and went back to Jasmine's house.

The place seemed strangely empty without Layla. Hungeringly empty as it always is when a familiar something or someone is no longer where it was. There is a haunting sense of wrongness, of things amiss. Here is a slot crying to be filled, and the one thing that will fill it will not.

Roaming restlessly from room to room, Michael kept listening for her, kept seeing her in his mind's eye. He could see her everywhere, the small irresistible, enchanting figure, the glossy tip-curling hair, the beautiful rose face, the small clean features, surged in captivated innocence. He could hear her voice everywhere; and always he, you, was in what she said . . . Did he want something? Was there something she could do for him? Was he all right? He must always tell her, please, if he wants anything.

'Are you feeling fine, yes? It would be terrible if I had hurt you.'

He started to enter the dining room, then came up short in the doorway. A table towel was draped over the table. Scrubbed, rinsed, and hung up to dry, but still faintly stained with the yellowishness of food sauce.

Michael swallowed painfully. Then, he dropped it into the laundry hamper and slammed down the lid.

The long hours appear to pass by slowly, hours that had always seemed short until today.

A little after nine thirty that night, Jasmine returned.

As usual, she left her troubles outside the door; came in with an eager smile on her face.

'Why, you're all dressed! How nice,' she said. 'Where's my girl, Layla?'

'She's not here,' Michael said. 'She--'

'Oh? Well, I guess I am a little late, and of course you're doing just fine.' She sat down, making motions of fanning herself. 'Whew, that awful traffic! I could make better time hopping on one foot.'

151

Michael paused, wanting to tell her, happy of anything that would let him wait.

'How's your arm, I mean your shoulder?'

'Okay,' she waved it carelessly. 'It looks like I'm branded for life, but at least it taught---me something. Keep away from knockers with cigars.'

'I think you should have it bandaged.'

'No can do. Have to dip in and out of my purse too much. Anyway, it's coming along all right.'

She expelled the subject carelessly, pleased but somewhat ashamed by his unusual concern. As the room grew silent, she took a cigarette from her purse; smiled merrily, as Michael hurried to light it.

'Hey, now, it looks like I really measured around here, doesn't it? A little more of this, and--What's that?'

She looked down at the bank notes he had dropped into her lap. Making a face, she raised her eyes.

'Fourteen thousand dollars,' he said. 'I hope it's enough to square us up, the hospital bills and all.'

'Well, sure. But you can't-- Oh,' she said tiredly. 'I guess you can, can't you? I hoped you were playing it straight, but I guess--'

'But you knew I wasn't,' Michael nodded. 'And now there's something else you've got to know. About Layla.'

Chapter 15

From Fairfax Coast a muted, gradually increasing shriek floated up to Jasmine's house, the sounds of the dinner hour and the early dawns of the nightclubs' day. Earlier, from about six until eight, there had been the racket of the business traffic: trucks, heavy and light pickups, making their last deliveries of the day and then turning tail toward the city; passenger cars, speeding and skidding and jockeying for position as they swarmed out from town to their own domains of towns, villages in that city. The cars were of all kinds, shapes, colors and sizes, from dragster on up, but there was an awesome abundance, even a predominance, at times of the upper-bracket makes. Caught now and then in the Strip's traffic, Michael had examined its content and, except for a few motorcycles and a Nissan, he had seen nothing, for as far as he could see, but Hondas, Toyota Lexus, Mitsubishi, and Hyundais.

Now, listening to the night's throbbing, Michael wished he was down there on the Strip, or practically any place but where he was. He had told Jasmine about Layla as quickly as he could, anxious to get it over with. But brushed over, it had probably sounded worse than in detail. He had felt the need to go back through it again, to explain just how what had led into what. But that seemed only to worsen matters, making him appear to pose as an honest if earthy young man who had been put to embarrassing disadvantage by the willful dizziness of a young woman.

There was just no good way of telling the story, he guessed. There simply wasn't, despite her definite open-mindedness and the fact she had never played the role of a true sister, as he saw it.

He gave a start as Jasmine's purse slid to the floor with a thwack. He bent forward to pick it up, then settled back uneasily as he saw what had fallen from the purse--a small, silencer-equipped handgun.

Her hand closed around it. She straightened again, hoisting it absently. Then, seeing his unease, her mouth twisted in a tight grin.

'Don't worry, Michael. It's an inclination, I'll admit, but it would cost me my permit.'

'Well, I wouldn't want you to do that,' Michael said. 'Not after the trouble I've already caused.'

'Oh, now, you shouldn't feel that way,' Jasmine said. 'You've paid your bill, haven't you?--tossed money at me like it was going out of style. You've explained and you've expressed regrets; you didn't really do anything to explain or make an apology for, did you? I was ignorant. She was simple minded--- slow enough to love and trust you, and to put the best possible explanation on what you did and said. We were misled, in other words, and it's a scammer's job to take the simpleton.'

'Have your own way about it,' Michael breaks in. 'I've made an apology, done everything I can. But if you want to get distasteful---'

'But I was always horrible, wasn't I? Always giving you a hard time. There was just no good in me, never ever. And you damned well couldn't miss a chance to get back at me!'

'Wh-aat?' He looked at her sharply. 'What the hell are you talking about?'

'The same thing you've spent your life sulking about and pitying yourself about, and needling me about. Because you had a hard time as a child. Because I didn't measure up to your standards of an older sisterhood.'

Michael blurted out sullenly that she hadn't measured up to anyone else's standards, either. Then, a little embarassed face, he tacked on a lukewarm renounce. 'Now, I don't really mean that, Jasmine; you just got me smart. Anyway, you've certainly done plenty out here, a lot more than I had any right to expect, and--'

'Never mind,' she cut him off. 'It wasn't enough. You've proved it wasn't. But there's a thing or two I'd like to get straight, Michael. To your way of thinking, I was a bad sister---yes, I was, so let's face it. But I ponder if it occurred to you that I didn't look at myself that way at all.'

'Well . . .' He paused. 'Well, no, I don't suppose you did.'

'It's all a matter of contrast, right? In the good community you were raised in, and built up against the other so-called sisters like friends you saw there, I was detestable. But I didn't grow up in that kind of environment, Michael. Where I was raised, a child was lucky if he got five years of school in his life. Lucky if he didn't die of rachitis or nematode or plain old starvation, or something worse. I can't remember a day, from the time I was old enough to remember anything, that I had enough to eat and didn't get a beating ----

Michael lit a cigarette, staring at her over the lighter; more irritated than concerned in what she was saying. What did it all amount to, anyway? Maybe she'd had a hard childhood in her primary school days, although he'd have to take her word for that. All he cared about was his own. But having had one, and knowing how it felt, why had she passed him the same kind of deal? She knew better. She hadn't been under the same ugly social pressures that had been brought to bear on her other families. Why, hell, she was living away from home at about the age he'd finished primary school!

Something about the last thought poked into him, cutting through the layered justifications which warmed him in their blooming glow while holding her off in outer darkness. Bitterly, he wondered just how soon he could decently break out of here. That was all he wanted. Not excuses, not explanations. Because of Layla, and because he did owe Jasmine something, he himself had been cast in the role of atoning and explainer. And, manfully, he had accepted it. But---

He became mindful at last that the room was silent. Had been silent for some time. Jasmine was leaning back in her chair, looking at him with a tiredly twisted smile.

'I seem to be keeping you up,' she said. 'Why don't you just run along and leave me to boil in my sins?'

'Now, Jasmine---' He made a defensive motion. 'You've never heard me dishonor you for anything.'

'But you have plenty to taint me for, don't you? It was pretty lousy of me to be a youngster at the same time you were. To act like a schoolgirl instead of a grown woman. Yes, sir, I was a real stinker not to grow up and act grown up as fast as you thought that I should.'

Michael was wounded. 'What do you want me to do?' he demanded. 'Pin a ring of light on you? You're doing a pretty good job of that yourself.'

'And making you look like a creep at the same time, hmm? But that's the way I am, you know; the way I've always been. Always picking on poor little Michael.'

'Oh, for crying out loud, Jasmine---!'

'Now, I've got just one more thing to say. I don't suppose it will do any good, but I've got to say it, anyway. Get out of the fraud, the swindler, the deceit, Michael. Get out right now, and stay out.'

'Why? Why don't you get out yourself?'

'Why?' Jasmine stared at him. 'Are you seriously asking me, _why?_ Why, you brainless weakling, big girl's blouse, milksop, I'd be dead if I even looked like I wanted out! It's been that way since I was seventeen years old. You don't get out of things like this---you're carried out!'

Michael wet his lips nervously. Maybe she wasn't emphasizing, although it was comforting to think that she must be. But he wasn't in her league, and he never would be.

'I'm strictly a smallt-con, Jasmine,' he said. 'Nothing but small-time stuff. I can walk away from it any time I want to.'

'It won't always be a small time. With you, it couldn't be. You're only twenty two years old, and already you can lay out fifty grand without turning a hair. You're only twenty two, and you've come up with a new angle on the chiseler---how to take blockheads for profit without changing hotels. So are you going to stop there?' Her head wagged in a stern negative. 'Huh-uh. The scamming is like everything else. You don't standstill. You either go up or down, usually down, but my brother Michael's going up.'

Michael was remorseful shamefacedly flattered. He pointed out that however it was, it was still the con. It didn't have the dangers that the organized rackets had.

'It doesn't, huh?' Jasmine asked. 'Well, you could have fooled me. Now, I heard of a guy just about your age who got hit so hard in the chest and side of his head that it almost killed him.'

'Well, uh--'

'Sure, sure, that doesn't count. That's different. And here's something else that's different.' She held up the burned hand. 'Do you know how I really got that burn? Well, I'll tell you . . .'

She told him, and he listened somewhat nauseated; shamed and embarrassed. Unwilling to associate such things with his sister, and unable to link them with himself. To that degree as he could, they tended to widen the rift that lay between him and Jasmine.

She saw how he felt; saw that it was no use. A slow anger welled through her tired body.

'So that's that,' she said, 'and it doesn't have anything to do with you, does it? Just another chapter in the dangers of Jasmine Chivers.'

'And very interesting, too,' he said, his voice light. 'Maybe you should write a book, Jasmine.'

'Maybe you should write one,' Jasmine said. 'Layla Ellis would make a quality chapter.'

Michael came stiffly to his feet. He nodded heartlessly, picked up his mobile phone and started toward the door; then paused with a motion of appeal. 'Jasmine,' he said, 'just what are you driving at, anyway? What more can I do about Layla?'

'You're asking me,' Jasmine said nastily. 'You've actually got the guts to stand there and ask me what you should do!'

'But---you're suggesting that I should marry her? Ask her to marry me? Oh, now, come off it! What kind of break would that be for her?'

'Oh, my God!, Jesus, Joseph, Mary,' Jasmine moaned.

Coloring, Michael slammed on his rucksack. 'I'm sorry I'm such a big disappointment to you. I'm going now.'

Jasmine looked at him, as he still paused, and remarked that she hadn't noticed. 'That's the second time you've fooled me tonight,' she said. 'Now you see him and now you don't see him, and when he goes nobody knows.'

He left suddenly.

Striding down the corridor, his steps slowed, and he paused; walking unsteadily on the point of turning back. At about the same point in time, Jasmine jumped up from her chair, started toward the door, and herself paused in staggering indecision.

They were so much alike, so much a part of one another. They were that close---for a moment.

The moment passed; a moment before murder. Then, flouting instinct, each made his decision. Each, as he always had, went his own way.

Chapter 16

Michael had his delayed dinner in an urban center restaurant. He ate hungrily, telling himself, and doubtless meaning it, that it was good to be eating in a swanky restaurant. It was what he was used to. The ultra-fine sameness of the food, whatever the restaurant, had a reassuring quality about it, not unlike a fast food burger joint. In its familiar and dependable nurture, it bolstered one's guided belief or principle that the more things changed the more they remained the same.

Similarly, it was good to be back in his own bed at the Park Royal. For here also would be his own bed wherever it was; standardized, always ready and waiting for him, simultaneously providing the pleasurable perquisites of permanence and impermanence. Perhaps, in his dreams, Layla briefly shared the bed with him, and he cringed, almost crying out. But there were entirely amenable spectres, also comfortably standardized, who came quickly to the rescue. They asked no more of him than he did of them, a sensual but spotless penetration which achieved its end without mental or moral involvement. One bathed quickly or lingeringly, bereft of the danger of nearing the water.

So, all in all, Michael Chivers slept well that night.

Awakening early, he lay for a while in the expected posture of all men awakening. Hands locked under his head, eyes gazing absently at the ceiling, letting his mind roam. Then, with a swift desertion of bed, he washed, dressed, and left the Park Royal.

He ate a hearty breakfast. He visited a hair salon, got a haircut , indulged himself in 'the works' and went back to his two-room suite. After showering, he put on completely fresh clothes, pimp or mafia lookin hat, shades, and shiny brogues included, and again left the holiday apartment..

He got his car from its parking lot, and turned it out into the traffic.

At first he felt a little awkward, nervous, after his very long absence from driving. But that passed quickly. In a few blocks he was himself again, moving the car along with instinctive ease, driving with the same unthinking skill that a secretary applies to a computer. He was part of this ocean of cars, aiding its sluggish movement and in turn aided by it. Without losing his identity, free to turn out of the flow when he chose, he still belonged to something.

Like many business organizations that had once been a traditional integrand of the urban city whole, the hiring house of marks & spencer's was now set down in a lovely residential district; sizably released, for a restless respite, from the stretched out giant which would inevitably surround it again. The firm was housed in a roomy cement, sand pebbles, and brick building, a lofty two story high for perhaps three fourths of its area. At the rear it projected up to a full story, thus accommodating the company offices.

Michael put his car on the private lot at the side of the building. Whistling absently, his eyes approving as he surveyed the familiar scene around him, he took his attache` from the car.

Someone else was looking them over too, he saw, but without his own carelessness. A young man---maybe, perhaps he wasn't quite so young, in long sleeves but wearing what looked like a stab proof vest. A law enforcement or security in appearance, he stood well back on the wide sidewalk encircling the building, looking seriously up and down and around, and occasionally jotting into a small notebook.

He turned and watched as Michael approached, his stare hardline at first, initially disapproving. Then, as Michael came on, determined, and smiled and nodded, 'Hello,' the stare registered a little warmth, and its proprietor nodded in return.

'Hello,' he said, almost as though the word demeaned him.

Michael passed on, smiling, mentally shaking his head.

A long, broad service counter stretched along the interior front of the building, breached at one end by a double door. Behind it, racks of stock-shelves ranged rearward, filling out neatly with the thousand and odd items which were wholesaled by various brands, and forming a baker's dozen parallel aisles.

It was early, and he was the only merchant peddler customer in the place. Normally at this hour, most of the cashiers were either having tea across the road or propped up along the counter in clusters, smoking and talking until they could resign themselves to the day. But there was no such cozyness nonsense this morning.

Everyone was present, without a cigarette, vapes, or tea carton in sight. The aisles hummed with activity: the pulling of orders, inventorying, restocking, dusting, and rearranging. Everyone was busy, or, much harder, pretending to be busy.

Through the years, he had become friendly with all of them, and all came forward for a handshake and a word of congratulation on his recovery. But they wasted no time on it. Confused, Michael turned to the cashier who was opening a catalogue for him.

'What's hit this place?' he asked. 'I haven't seen anyone as busy since the place caught fire.'

'Mr Senior hit it, that's what!'

'Mr Senior? Is that anything like the rush waste product?'

The cashier laughed sinisterly. 'You can say that again! Brother,' he brushed imaginary sweat from his brow. 'If that sleazebag stays around much longer---!'

Senior, he elaborated, was one of the Headquarters big shots, a seeming mixture of financial officer, efficiency expert, and jack-of-all-trades. 'Came out here right after you went into the hospital---one of those university bully thugs, he looks like. And he ain't had a kind word for anyone. Ain't no one knows anything but him, and everyone's either a terrific or a bum. Now, you know that's not so, Michael. You won't find a harder-working, more efficient group of lads anywhere than we got right here!'

'That's right,' Michael nodded agreeably, although it was very far from right. 'Maybe he'll run me off, do you suppose?'

'I was going to tell you. He did chop off several of the salesmen; just won't wholesale to them any more. And what kind of sense does that make? They're all selling on commission. If they don't sell, they don't make anything, so---shhh, here he comes!'

As Michael had suspected, the financial officer, jack-of-all-trades, was the censorious looking young man he had seen outside the building. A split second after the cashier had spoken, he was upon them, shooting out his hand like a weapon.

'Senior. Headquarters,' he said. 'Nice to meet you.'

'This is Mr. Chivers,' the cashier said, nervously dutiful. 'Michael's one of our best salesmen, Mr. Senior.'

'He is the best.' Senior didn't give the cashier a peek. 'Which isn't saying much for this place. Want to talk to you, Chivers.'

He turned, still clinging to Michael's hand as though to hustle him along. Michael remained where he was, pulling Senior back around with a jerk. He smiled pleasantly, as the headquarters man blinked at him, startled.

'That was a pretty backhanded compliment, Mr. Senior,' he said, 'and I never let people get away with things like that. If I did, I wouldn't be a good salesman.'

Senior considered the statement; nodded with sharp prudentness. 'You're right. I apologize. Now, I'd still like to talk to you.'

'Lead the way,' Michael said, picking up his attache`.

Mr Senior led him back down the counter, suddenly swerving away from the double doors and moving toward the building entrance. 'How about some tea or coffee, okay? Set a bad example; too much trifling around here already. But it's hard to talk with so many people trying to listen in.'

'You don't seem to think much of them,' Michael remarked.

Senior said crisply, as they started across the road, that he had no feelings at all about impressionistic people. 'It depends on how they mass up. If they're on the ball, I've got plenty of consideration for them.'

In the restaurant, he asked for a small amount of milk as well as coffee, spooned with two teaspoons of sugar mixing the three together a little at a time as he sipped from his cup. 'Festers,' he explained. 'Your trouble too, right?' Then, without waiting for an answer he went on:

'Had you spotted me when you passed me this morning, Chivers. Nothing unmethodical or unsystematic about you. Looked like you were going somewhere and you knew the way. Figured then that you must be Chivers; connected you with your sales right away. And when I said that it didn't say much for Marks and Spencer's---your being the best man, I mean---I meant just that. You mass up as a top-flight man in my book, but you've had no impetus here. No one is walking on your heels. Just a lot of uncoordinated, so the aptness was not to stretch yourself. I'm bouncing the laggards, incidentally. Makes no difference to me if they are only on commission. If they're not making good money, they're not giving us good representation and we can't afford to have them around. What's your selling experience, anyway? Before you came here, I mean?'

'Selling's all I've done since I left secondary school,' Michael said, not knowing what all this was leading up to but willing to go along for the ride. 'You name it, I've sold it. All door-to-door stuff. Premiums, brushes, bath soaps, lagers.'

'You're singing my song,' Senior grinned crookedly. 'I'm the guy who worked his way through university peddling subscriptions. You switched to business house selling when you came with us; why?'

'It's easier to get into doors,' Michael said, 'and you can build up regular customers. The knocking, and doorbell ringing from house to house stuff is mostly one-shot.'

Senior nodded approvingly. 'Ever supervise salesmen? You know; kind of head them up, keep them on their toes.'

'I've run door to door crews,' Michael snatched. 'Who hasn't?'

'I haven't. Don't have the talent for it, somehow.'

'Or diplomacy?' Michael smiled.

'Or diplomacy. But never mind me; I do all right. The point is, this store needs a sales manager. Should have had one right along. Someone who's proved he's a salesman and can handle other salesmen. He'd have a lot of muck to clear out, or put some vigor back into them. Hire new men, and give them a good draw if they cut the stuff. What do you think?'

'I think it's a good idea,' Michael said.

'Now, I don't know offhand what your best year's earnings have been. Around a hundred thousand, I believe. But put it this way. We'll top your best year by twenty-five thousand; make it thirty thousand in round numbers. That's just the starters, of course. Give you a year at one hundred thirty, and if you're not worth a lot more than that by then I'll kick you the hell out. But I know you will be worth more. Knew you were my kind of man from the minute I saw you this morning. And now that we've got that settled, I'm going to help myself to one of your cigarettes and have a sweet cup of tea, and if my stomach doesn't like it I'll kick it the hell out, too.'

Michael held out his cigarette package. In the swift-fire delivery of Mr Senior talk, he had let its meaning slip away from him. And coming to him suddenly, hitting him like a blow, his hand gave a spasmodic tug.

Senior looked at him, blinking. 'Something wrong? By a twist of fate, don't cigarettes and sweet tea bother you? Your ulcers, I mean.'

Michael nodded, shook his head. 'I, uh, it wasn't a bad ulcer. Just happened to be in a bad place. Struck a vein. I---look, Mr. Senior---'

'Cheer up, Michael. Cheer up for heaven sake, and smile when you say that. How old are you, Michael? Twenty-one or two? Fine. No reason at all why you can't.'

Michael's mind raced seriously. A sales manager! Him, Michael Chivers, defrauder de luxe, a sales manager! But he couldn't be, damnit! It would be too confining, too proscribed. He would lose the freedom of movement necessary to carry on the scamming. The job itself, the importance of it, would preclude any such activities. As a commission salesman, he might reasonably loiter in the places where the evil scams could be practiced. But as the company's sales manager---no! The slightest boom would dump him cold.

He couldn't take the job. On the other hand, how could he turn it down, without arousing suspicion? How could you reasonably refuse a job that was right up your alley, one that was not only much better than the one you had but promised to become far, far better?

'Glad to get this thing settled, Michael,' Mr Senior was saying. 'Now, we've wasted enough time here, so if you're through with your Latte`.'

'Mr. Senior,' Michael said. 'I can't take the job. I can't take it right away, I mean. This is the first day I've been up and around, and I just dropped by to say hello and---'

'Oh?' Senior looked at him judiciously. 'Well, you do look a little pale. How soon will you be ready, a few days?'

'Well, I---the doctor's checking me over in a couple days time, but I'm not sure that---'

'One full week then. Or take a little longer if you have to. Be plenty of work, and you've got to be in shape for it.'

'But you need a sales manager right now! It wouldn't be fair to you to---'

'I take care of the being-fair-to-me department.' Senior permitted himself a cold grin. 'Things have been going to hell this long. They can go a little longer.'

'Only---'

But there was nothing more to say. Perhaps he could think of an out for himself during the next few days or so, but none occurred to him straight away.

They walked back across the road together, and then he went on by himself to his car. He got into it uncertainly, started the motor, then cut it off again.

What now? How could he pass the time that senior had given him? Selling was out of the question, of course, since he was supposedly unready to work. But there was the other, his real occupation; the source of the wealth behind the four harlequin pictures.

He started the car again. Then, with a frustrated groan, he again shut it off. Since work was out, so also was the scam, or perhaps he could take his chance. He wouldn't dare turn a trick. Not before the next couple of days, at least, when he would normally be lazy and could unsuspiciously wallow in some gambole prance.

A couple of days. And this was only Tuesday.

He thought about Emily. With an unconscious growl, he dismissed her from his mind. Not today. It was too soon after Layla.

Starting his car for the third time, he drove around for a few hours, then had lunch at a drive-in and returned to the Park Royal. He spent a restless early evening reading crime books. He had a huge dinner, and killed the evening at the theatre.

Faced with more idleness the following morning, he was again moved to call Emily But somehow, without seeming to think about it, he rang Layla's number instead.

Coming to the phone in a tired voice, she said she could not see him. They had no reason to see each other.

'Oh, now, we might have,' he said. 'Why don't we get together and talk about it?'

She paused. 'About what, exactly?'

'Well---you know. A lot of things. We'll have lunch, and---'

'No,' she said sternly. 'No, Michael. It is impossible, anyway. I am working regularly at the hospital now. Late shifts. And I must sleep.'

'This evening, then.' Suddenly it had become very important that he linked up with her to make amends. 'Before you go to work. Or I can pick you up in the morning, after you finish. I---.'

He hurried on. He had a new job, he explained. Or, well, he was thinking about taking a new job. He wanted her opinion on it, and---

'No,' she said. 'No, Michael.'

And she hung up.

Chapter 17

His face was a little long, his mouth wide and a trifle thin-lipped, his eyes gray and wide set. His dark hair was very curly on top. He got useful intelligence about a huge cash drop off, at a grocery store in Dennery. Evil thoughts raced through Michael's mind about the huge loot, until he felt quite rested and high spirited.

Mr Harper did not become a multi-millionaire through share-honesty; he had a bit of evil ways about him where a large amount of money was concerned.

Michael talked to Mr Harper about the intelligence of the large loot, even though Michael had just recovered from his illness, money had no limits for him he was greedy. He would take the sales manager job Mr Senior offered him, as a front, as a means to cover his tracks. Mr Harper gave him the advice. However, he wanted a percentage of the heist. He even advises Michael about an undercover store to pick up a rifle for the job, providing he could keep his trap shut should the plan fail.

His dark sweater snugly emphasized his athletic rugby player physique shoulders and biceps, the flaring fullness below it and the rich contours above. A security cap was cocked partly on his head. His army shoes laced to his ankles tapered up into a pair of slacks which were really much less than skintight, although they did seem pretty well filled to capacity in at least one area.

He looked heartbreakingly young and evil. He looked---well, what was wrong with the word---evil? Tingling pleasantly, Michael decided there was nothing at all wrong with it.

He began his journey in a hired car driving slowly, to glance more and more frequently at the dashboard clock and the speedometer's mileage indicator.

Michael took another look at the clock, drove still more slowly. At the start of a slope he stopped the car and began raising the canvas top. A lorry and a few cars went past, the driver of one slowing as though to offer help. Michael waved them on in a way to let them know that she meant it, then slid back behind the wheel.

He lit a cigarette, flipped it away after a few puffs, and stared narrowly through the windshield. He was patient, he was calm, no partners, the three of the best remedies you needed when pulling off a heist, there would be no one to inform on you, no one to double back and rob you of your share or percentage of the robbery..

In any event, Michael never made any last-minute changes in plans. If changes seemed indicated, he simply dropped the job, either permanently or until a later date.

Michael started the car once more

The stock and barrel of a rifle were slung on loops inside his overcoat. Michael took them out, hung the coat back in the closet, and began to assemble them. The stock was from a top notch twenty-two rifle. The barrel, as well as the rest of the gun proper, had either been made or made over by Mr Harper's friends.

Michael slid a twenty-two slug into the breechloader, closed and locked it and rocked the slug into place. He began to pump, pumping harder as the resistance inside the air chamber grew. When he could no longer depress the plunger, he gave it several quick turns, sealing the end of the cylinder.

He smoked a cigarette and scanned the daily newspaper which Mr Harper had brought with his suggestion of a successful robbery, pausing now and then to pick idly at any developing gossip.

When he reached the north-west coast, he would need to hole up temporarily; to reconnoiter, switch cars and break trail generally, before jumping into Castries. It was wise to do that at any rate, even though it might not be absolutely necessary. And Mr Harper had lined up a place where he could take temporary sanctuary. It was a small tourist area, owned by some distant relatives of his. They were naturalized citizens, an almost painfully honest, elderly couple. But they had an unreasonable fear of the law enforcement team, brought with them from the old country, and they were even more terrified of Mr Harper. So, reluctantly, they had submitted to his demands, on this occasion and several others.

Michael was confident that he could handle them quite well without Mr Harper's further assistance. He was confident that they would be even more rather than less cooperative if they knew that he had the cold killer instinct inside him.

Staring at his watch, Michael was tempted to light another cigarette, but instead he picked up the rifle. Standing back in the concealing shadows of a nearby room, he took aim through the window, one eye squinted. The security guard was due at the main entrance any minute now.

The security guard was just stepping across the bank's threshold, and had almost disappeared into its dark interior. Michael triggered the gun and there was a stinging, whisper sound, like the sudden emission of breath.

He didn't wait to see the security guard fall; when Michael shot at something he hit it. With a more powerful rifle his aim would have been just as accurate at two hundred yards as it had been at twenty.

Michael reloaded the rifle, and again pumped up the pressure. He unfastened the stock, locked it up in his briefcase, and put the rest back in the loops of the overcoat. He picks up the shell casings and puts them into his overcoat pocket, so there'll be no ballistic results.

He lifted the coat out, draped it loosely over one arm. He walked back and forth with it for a moment, then nodded with satisfaction and hung it back up. Mr Harper's friend wouldn't expect him to return the rifle. It would come as a complete surprise to him. But just in case it didn't----

I'll think of something, Michael assured himself. And went to work on the more immediate problem.

He scrubbed his hands in the store washrooms and turned down the turned up cuffs of his shirt. For no conscious reason, Micharl sighed.

He'd never been on any tough jobs than this one, but never one where so much depended on its success. Everything he had was on the line here; everything that he wanted. He was twenty two.

The thoughts stirred murkily in the bottom of his mind. Neglected and unadmitted; appeared only in an unconscious sigh.

He'd had work to do, and there'd been no point in looking. If there was more trouble, he'd be able to hear it.

Now, however, he looked again. Michael winced and shook his head, unconsciously as he had sighed.

It was a minute and a half that ticked by, he needed to speed up the heist process. Michael adjusted his tie and put on his suit jacket. He went down the dull crimson carpet to the end of the hall, then turned left into a short side corridor. A hard plastic trash can stood between the back steps and the side-alley window. His luck was far better than he could have hoped for.

A stake bed delivery truck was parked rear end first at the curb. Next to it was a toyota, its windows wind up tightly. But next to them, parked to the windward of them, was another van loaded almost to the level of the shop's ground floor windows.

He was ready to admit that his groggy faith was a personal thing. As a professional criminal, he had schooled himself against placing complete trust in anyone. And as a criminal, he had learned to link infidelity with treachery. It revealed either a dangerous flaw in character, or an equally dangerous shift in loyalties. In any case, the robbing partner was a bad risk in a game where no risk could be condoned.

Michael loaded the two money cases into the car. And the dead security guard wrapped up in plastic in the car booth. He made a U-turn, honking for a couple of country dwellers to get out of the way, and headed out of town.

A few miles away, Michael grinning meanly to himself . He dumped the security guard body into a high current infested alligator river. And dismantled and ditch the rifle a further miles away into a scrap yard skip.

Mr Harper asked him how he had made out.

'Two millions in banknotes. Maybe four million in cash, Michael wasn't quite sure. He knew it was a lot of dough.'

'Around two or perhaps four million?' Mr Harper's eyes flicked at him. 'I see. Must've been a lot of fifties and hundred.'

'So maybe there's more, dammit! You think I figured it out on an adding machine?

So---The thought came to Michael's mind.

'I guess I shouldn't have killed the security guard, should Harper? It's going to make things tough for me.' The guard's death was regrettable but unavoidable; when an accessory to a crime collapsed so completely, there was nothing to do but kill him.

Michael dumped the car at Mr Harper's friend's scrapyard to be crushed first thing in the morning. Michael drove another hired car from another associate of Mr Harper, it was a very nice Lexus leather seated with all the electric buttons inside; and then they were on their way to Castries.

A couple of hours driving got them off of the country roads and back onto the highway. They paused there briefly to consult their road maps, a sat nav or dashcam is not a wise idea to leave on or use when committing crimes. Picking out the most concealed route to Castries City. The town was further to the north, further rather than nearer their concluding destination. But that, of course, was its advantage. It was the last place they would be expected to go. As a jumping-off place, it offered no clue as to what their destination might be.

Their plan was to abandon the car as soon as they reached Castries and take a taxi to a small guesthouse.They both laughed in a spiteful manner.

Mr Harper bit his lip,as they entered the city of Castries. He remained where he was for a moment, and then, with a kind of dreary nonchalance, he walked around the pavement and moved around the palms.

It was around four o'clock in the morning, Mr Harper decided to open the mini bar drawn up in front of Michael. Silently he sat down at Michael's side, and silently he fixed him a drink, his evil eyes warmly congratulating him. 'This was a pretty good job Michael. I'm sure the corrupt law enforcement team will see us through this.'

'Oh, well,' Michael sighed. 'I hope so, Harper.'

'I don't care about myself. I've been told off by my sister Jasmine Michael. But someone like you, someone that everyone has always liked and respect----'

Mr Harper turned to Michael with thoughtful admiration. 'Do you know,' he said, 'I believe you're really made for stepping into the big time.'

Michael nodded to some degree. He refilled their glasses. On the wall a little chime began to toll the hour of five o'clock in the early morning. And in Michaels brain a band struck up the strains of _Home Sweet Home_.

'Well,' Micahel said. 'I guess the successful heist is just about over, Harper.'

'Yes,' Mr Harper said. 'Just about over, Michael.'

'Let's toast our glass Mr. Harper! To become rich! To you and our successful getaway!'

Chapter 18

On the following day, he called Emily Casey. But there again he was defeated. He was amazed as well as annoyed, since, for a moment, she had seemed to welcome an early start on their Laguna beach, back-pedalling herself in practically the same breath. It couldn't be done, she explained. At least, due to delicate womanly reasons, a cyclic difficulty, it wouldn't be very practical. Another day? Mmm, no, she was afraid not. But the next day, maybe, or---should be fine.

Michael suspected that she was simply a little offended at him; that this was his retribution for his weeks of idleness. Certainly, however, he was of no mind to plead with her, so he said casually that a couple days from now would be fine with him, too, and the arrangements were made on that basis.

He killed the rest of the day happily now being a millionaire or most part of it, with a trip to the Marigot Bay beaches. The next day, he was free to get some much needed rest or more scamming. But after some mental uncertainty, he decided against it.

Let it go. He wasn't quite in the frame of mind. He needed to snap out of himself a little more,
to jerk off certain disturbing memories which might add to the dangers of a profession which already had enough perils.

He wasted time aimlessly through the day, he became thoughtful; almost, he pitied himself. What a way to live, he thought with a feeling of bitterness. Always watching every word he said, carefully scrutinizing every word. And never making a move that wasn't studiously examined in advance. Descriptively, he walked through life on a high wire, and he could turn his mind from it only at his own danger.

Of course, he was well-paid for his efforts, his robberies, his scammings. The loot had piled up fast, and it would go on piling up. But there was the trouble---it simply piled up! As useless to him as so many takeaway brochures.

Needless to say, this state of things would not go on forever; he would not forever live a second-class life in the Park Royal. In another two years, his defrauding loot would total enough for retirement, and he could drop caution with the scamming which impelled it. But those two years were necessary to insure retirement, filling it with all the things he had been forced to forego. And just suppose he didn't live another two years. Or even one year. Or even one month.

The languishing exhausted itself. And him, as well. The seemingly endless day passed, and he fell asleep. And then, toppingly, it was morning. Then, at last, he had something to do.

They were making the trip by stagecoach, the eastbound twelve o'clock, and Emily was meeting him at the coach station. Michael parked his car on the car park lot, he would hire another for their holiday use, and took his bag out of the trunk.

It was only fifteen minutes after eleven, a little bit too early to expect Emily. Michael bought their tickets, gave the seat numbers and his bag to a well-tipped smartly dressed coach worker, and entered the station bar.

He had a coffee, stretching it out as he glanced occasionally at the clock. At fifteen minutes to one, he got up from his stool and went back through the entrance.

The eastbound was always crowded, carrying not only the civilian traffic but the swarms of holiday makers and engineers returning to their duty stations at the power station plant. Michael watched as they streamed through the numbered gates and down the long ramps which led to the stagecoaches. A little tense, he again checked the time.

Ten minutes until midday. That was enough time, of course, but not too much. The station was more than a block in depth, and the coach ramp was practically a block long. If Emily didn't get here very quickly, she might as well stay home.

Four minutes until midday.

Three minutes.

Bitterly, Michael gave up and started back to the bar. She wouldn't do this intentionally, he was sure. Probably, she'd been caught up in a traffic jam, one of the Sicklers of gridlock cars which afflicted the city's supposedly high speed, super highway. But, blast it, if she'd ever start any place a little early, instead of waiting until the last minute---!

He heard his name called.

He turned and saw her coming through the entrance, scurrying behind the uniformed staff who carried her luggage. The male staff glared a smile at Michael as he passed. 'Do my best, mister. Just you stay behind me.'

Michael grabbed Emily and hurried her along with him.

'Sorry,' Emily wheezed. 'Darned apartment house! Traffic jam, and---'

'Never mind. Save your gasp,' Michael said.

They raced the shine-floored length of the building, passed through the gate and on down into the seemingly endless stretch of ramp. At its far end a coach conductor stood, watch in hand. As they approached, he pocketed the watch, and started up the short side ramp to the loading platform.

They followed him, passed him.

As the stagecoach pulled out, they huff and puff.

They dropped in their seats. Breathless, they slumped into them. And for the next ten minutes, they hardly stirred.

At last, as they were pulling out of the town, Emily's head turned on the half leath-slipped seat back and she grinned at him.

'You're a good man, Michael.'

'And you're a good woman, Miss Emily Casey,' he said.

Emily gave him a hard look.

'I'm going to call the conductor,' she declared.

'I couldn't buy your silence with a drink?'

'The silence, I'll buy a couple of hours of it, after that. You buy the drink, and be sure you rinse your mouth out with it.'

Michael laughed. 'I'll wait for you if you like.'

'Go on then,' Emily said searingly, closing her eyes and leaning back against the seat.   Michael patted her on the shoulder. Rising, he walked the few steps down to the lower deck to the mini bar-lounge. He was feeling up to the mark again, back in form. The sulk about what to do with the million banknotes he stole, introspectiveness of recent days had slipped from him, and he felt like rocking.

As he had expected, the stagecoach minibar was busy. Unless he could squeeze in with some excuse, which was what he intended to do, there was no place to stand.

He surveyed the scene respectively, then turned to the attendant behind the small bar. 'I'll have a merlot and water,' he said.

'Sorry, sir. Can't serve you unless you're seated.'

'Let's see. How much is it, anyway?'

'Eighty-five cents, sir. But I can't---'

'Forty dollars,' Michael nodded, laying two twenty bills on the counter. 'Exact change, right?'

He got his drink. Glass in hand, he started up the short steps, swaying occasionally with the movement of the stagecoach. Halfway down the aisle, he allowed himself to be swayed against a booth where three engineer men sat, jolting their drinks and tilting a little of his own on the table.

He apologized profusely. 'You've got to let me buy you a round. No, I insist. Waiter!'

Extremely pleased, they persuade him to sit down, squeezing over to make room. The drinks came, and disappeared. Over their protests, he bought another round.

'But it ain't fair, pal. We're buying next time.'

'No sweat,' Michael said pleasantly. 'I'm not sure I can drink another one, but----'

He broke off, glimpsing down at the floor. He moaned, squinted. Then, stooping, he reached slightly under the booth. And straightening again, he dropped a small dotted cube on the table.

'Did one of you guys drop this?' he asked.

The tat rolled. The bets doubled and redoubled. With the deceptive swiftness of the stagecoach, the stack of money streamed into Michael Chivers's pockets. When his three misguided stooges thought about him later, it would be as a 'hell of a nice guy,' so harmonious troubled by his unwanted and unintended winnings as to make shameful any troubled thought of their own. When Michael thought about them later, however, he would not. All his thinking was concentrated on them, the time of their fleecing; in keeping them constantly diverted and disarmed. And in the high intensity of that concentration, in fueling its hot flames, he had nothing of them left for afterthoughts. They enjoyed their drinks; his were tasteless. Occasionally, one of them went to the toilet; he could not. Now and then, they looked out the window, remarking on the beauty of the passing scenery for it was beautiful with the golden sand, picturesque beaches, the green and gold of the groves, the white villas with red-tiled roofs: strikingly reminiscent of St. Kitts. But while Michael sounded in with appropriate comments, he did not look where they looked or see what they saw.

At last, swarming up out of his concentration, he saw that the seats had emptied, and that the stagecoach was creeping through the industrial outskirts of eastbound, the terminus of the coach trip. Rising, wringing hands all around with the servicemen, he turned to leave the bar-lounge. And there was Emily smiling at him from its head.

'Thought I'd better come looking for you,' she said. 'Have fun?'

'Oh, you know. Just rolling for drinks,' he shrugged. 'Sorry I left you alone for so long.'

'Forget it,' she smiled, taking his arm. 'I didn't mind a bit.'

Chapter 19

Michael hired a car at Mon Repos, and they drove out to their beach hotel. It sat in a deep lawn, high on a bluff overlooking the Atlantic. Emily was delighted with it. Breathing in the clean cool air, she insisted on a brief tour of the grounds before they went inside.

'Now, this is something like,' she declared. 'This is living!' And sliding a steamy glance at him. 'I don't know how I'll show my gratitude.'

'Oh, I'll think of something,' Michael said.

He registered for them, and they followed the attender upstairs. Their rooms were on opposite sides of a corridor, and Emily looked at him puzzlingly, demanding an explanation.

'Why the apartheid bit?' she said. 'Not that I can't stand it, if you can.'

'I thought it would be better that way, separate rooms under our own names.Just in case there's any scuffling, you know.'

'Why should there be any scuffling?'

Michael said easily that there shouldn't be any; there was no reason why there should be. 'But why take chances? After all, we're right across from each other. Now, if you'd like me to show you how convenient it is----'

He pulled her into his arms, and they stood locked together for a while. But when he started to take it from there, she pulled away.

'Later, hmm?' She stopped before the mirror, idly prinking at her hair. 'I hurried so fast this morning that I'm only half-put together.'

'Later it is,' Michael nodded agreeably. 'Like something to eat now, or would you rather wait for dinner?'

'Oh, dinner by all means. I'll give you a call.'

He left her, still stopped before the mirror, and crossed to his own room. Unpacking his bag, he decided that she was interested rather than annoyed about the separate rooms, and that, in any case, the arrangement was compulsory. He was known as a single man. Departing from that singleness, he would have to use an assumed name. And where then was his protective front, so carefully and painfully built up through the years?

He was bound to the front, bound to and bound by it. If Emily was provoked or vex, then she could simply get over being provoked or vex. He wished he hadn't had to explain to her, since explanations were always bad. He also regretted that she had seen him operating in the club car. But the wish and the regret were small things, idly reflective rather than daunting.

Anyone might do a little gambling for drinks. Anyone might be cautious about hotel registrations. Why should Emily regard the first as a professional activity, and the second as a cover for it, a front which must always ensue to him like a shadow?

Unpacked, Michael stretched out on the bed, surprisingly grateful for the chance to rest. He had not realized that he was so tired, that he could be so glad to lie down. Apparently, he reflected, he was still not fully recovered from the effects of his past two nights.

Soothed by the distant throb of the ocean, he fell into a comfortable nap, awakening just before nightfall. He stretched lazily and sat up, unconsciously smiling with the pleasure of his comfort. Salt-scented air wafted in through the windows. Far off to the coastline, beneath a pale sky, an orange-red sun sank slowly into the ocean. Several times he had seen the sun set off the Southeastern coast, but each time was a new experience. Each sunset seemed more beautiful than the last.

Reluctantly, as the mobile phone rang, he turned away from its splendor. Emily's voice came merrily over the line.

'Boo, you young man! Are you buying me dinner or not?'

'Absolutely not,' he said. 'Give me one good reason why I should.'

'Can't. Not over the phone.'

'Excuses,' he moaned. 'Always excuses! Well, okay, but it's strictly steak pies.'

They had cocktails on the hotel's patio bar. Then, driving farther on into the city, they ate at a seafood restaurant jutting out over the ocean. Emily had stated a truce with her diet, and she proved that she meant it.

The meal opened with a prawn cocktail, practically a meal in itself. Served with hot ciabatta-bread and a fresh garnish salad, the main course was a sizzling platter of assorted seafoods bordered by a rim of onion rings, potato chips, and coleslaw. Then came dessert, a strawberry cheesecake, and pots of tea.

Emily sighed happily as she accepted a cigarette. 'As I said earlier, this is living! I honestly don't think I can move!'

'Then, of course you don't feel like discoing.'

'Crazy,' she said. 'Whatever gave you an idea like that?'

She loved dancing, and she shook a leg very well; as, for that matter, did he. More than once, he caught the eyes of other guests on them; seeing them also, Emily pressed closer to him, bending her flexible body to his.

After perhaps an hour of dancing, when the floor became oppressively crowded, they went for a moonlight drive up the coast, turning around and heading back to the city of Oceanside. The mounting waves of the night tide foamed with phosphorus. They came rolling in from the distant depths of the ocean, striking against the shore in a steady series of thunder-like roars. On the rocky outcrops of the shore, an occasional seal gleamed.

It was almost ten when Michael got them back to their hotel, and Emily was suppressing a snooze. She apologized, saying it was the weather, not the company. But when they again stood in front of their rooms, she held out her hand in good night.

'You don't mind, do you, Michael? It's been such a wonderful evening, I guess I just wore myself out.'

'Of course you did,' he said. 'I'm pretty tired myself.'

'You're sure now? You're sure you don't mind?'

'Beat it,' he said, pushing her through her door. 'It's okay.'

But of course it wasn't okay, and he minded a great deal. He entered his own room, restraining an angry impulse to slam the door. Taking off his clothes, he sat down on the edge of the bed; puffed gloomily at a cigarette. A hell of a holiday, this was! It would serve her right if he walked out on her!

The mobile phone rings faintly. It was Emily. She spoke with pent-up laughter.

'Open your door.'

'What?' He grinned expectantly. 'What for?'

'Open it and find out, you saphead!'

He hung up and opened his door. There was a hissing sound, 'Gangway! from the door opposite his. And he stood back. And Emily came skipping across the hallway. Her black hair stood in a tranquil pile on her head. She was completely naked. Gravely, a finger under her chin, she curtsied before him.

'I hope you don't mind, young man,' she said. 'I just washed my clothes, and I couldn't do a thing with them.'

Then, babbling, choking with laughter, she collapsed in his arms. 'Oh, you!' she catches her breath. 'If you could have seen your face when I told you good night! You looked s--so---so--_ah, ha, ha---'

He picked her up and tossed her on the bed.

Michael stood quite motionless, and he knew what had happened to him. Under Emily's touch his manhood was raised quite stiffly. 'Now come on,' he heard Emily whisper softly. He saw how she threw herself around on the bed, lifted her by the waist and put her legs to spread. At that moment, she already felt his fingers between her legs. Quite willingly Emily lay back on the bed in a more comfortable position, and Michael rubbed his stiff member against her honeypot lips. Emily rose up, and he now showed her his manhood which she calmly took in her hand. Then Emily pulled back the foreskin, and she saw the glans appear. She now pushed the foreskin a few times back and forth, played with it, and rejoiced when the glans, like the rosy head of a small animal peeked out.

With the left hand played Michael on a nipple of Emily, which became higher and more pointed. Suddenly Michael lowered his head, grabbed the breast of Emily and began to work on her nipple. Lick and put it in his mouth for some hard suck, just like he always does. Emily cried and wailed with lust:

Michael pulled her close, kissed her stormily, picked and played with his fingers on her clitoris some more. He entered her hard but slowly 'Jesus, Joseph, Mary, you're kicking my stomach in'. Michael made no answer but thrust only ever harder his manhood all the way in her belly, so that every time she gave a jolt. She began to snap, gasp, and at last uttered a low growl that sounded like a cry. Her breath was whistling, she threw so that now her buttocks are in the air, floated over the manhood. He held her by the buttocks tightly and drilled into her and moaned only once: 'Now.' With that he rams his long, broad manhood into her again so deep into her body that she roared aloud with delight.

And he showed himself so expertly and talented in drilling, pushing and sharpening, so that the bed under the weight of it and Emily began to puff loudly----, now ----, now----.' That was all that was said. But Emily suddenly felt something deep inside her, hot and knew that he was now splashing. His manhood jerked and spasmed, his fingers dug into her shoulder like a wild cat and there was one hot wave after the other, which she gave way in her body like the touch of a wet tip of his tongue.

She also huffed, groaned, moaned and pinched their butt together. When Michael let go of her and she straightened up, the juice flowed out of her honeypot, it flowed down her thighs so that she was quite wet. She felt his prick still influenced her, had a little pain and was quite dizzy from the great excitement.

Chapter 20

But afterward, after Emily had gone back to her own room, depression came to him and what had seemed like such a hell of a time became distasteful, even a little disgusting. It was the depression of overfill the tail of complacency's kite. You flew high, wide, and handsome, imposing on the breeze that might have wafted you along indefinitely; and then it was gone, and down, down, down you went.

Rolling restlessly in the dark hotel room, Michael told himself that the gloom was natural enough and a small enough price to pay for what he had received. But as to the last, at least, he was not convinced. There was too much of a sameness about the evening's delights. He had been on the same route too many times. He'd been there before, too double-damned often, and however you traveled, backward, forward, or walking on your hands, you always got to the same place. You got nowhere, in other words, and each trip took a little more out of you.

Up to the present times, did he really want anything changed? Even now, in his misery, weren't his thoughts already reaching out and across the hall?

He flung his legs over the side of the bed and sat up. Lighting a cigarette, pulling a gown around his shoulders, he sat looking out into the moonlit night. Thinking that perhaps it wasn't him or them, he or Emily, that had brought him to this shadowy despair. Perhaps it was a combination of things.

He didn't have his full strength back yet. He'd used up a lot of energy in catching the stagecoach earlier in the day. And swindling after so long an idleness had been unusually tightening on him. Then there'd been a lot of little things, Emily's oddness about the separate rooms, for example. And that heavy dinner, at least twice as much as he needed or wanted. Then, after all that----.

His mind went back to the dinner now, the large quantity and richness of it. And suddenly the cigarette tasted very bad to him, and a wave of sickness surged up through his stomach. He ran to the bathroom, a hand over his mouth, cheeks swelled out. And he got there barely in time.

He rid himself of the meal, every dejected mouthful of it. He rinsed out his mouth with warm salted water, then drank a bottle of cold water. And immediately he began spewing up again.

Bending over the sink, he anxiously studied his stomach's washings, and to his relief he found them clear. There was no revealing trace of purple-brown that would signify internal bleeding.

Trembling a little, he had a quick shower, he wobbled back to bed and pulled the covers over him. He felt a lot better now, lighter and cleaner. He closed his eyes, and was swiftly asleep.

He slept soundlessly, dreamlessly; seeming to compress a couple hours of sleep in one. Awakening at about seven o'clock, he knew he'd had his limit and that further sleep was out of the question.

He shaved, took a long shower and dressed. That took more than a half-hour, trawling it out as he would. So there it was, only seven forty-five in the morning, and he was as much at loose ends as if he was back in Castries.

Certainly, he couldn't call Emily at such an hour. Emily had indicated last night that she intended to sleep until late morning, and that she would joyfully slaughter anyone who awakened her before then. At any rate, he was in no hurry at all to see Emily. It was labor enough to pull himself together again, without the necessity of entertaining her.

Going down to the hotel diner, he had some toast and sweet tea. But he only did it as a matter of routine, of character. Regardless of the night before, a man ate breakfast in the morning. He ate, hungry or not, or else he inevitably found himself in trouble.

Walking down a graveled surface to the rock face above the ocean, he let his eyes wander aimlessly over the expanse of sea and sand: The frigid-looking whitecaps, the blinking, faraway sails of boats, the sweeping, constantly searching gulls. Bareness. Eternal, infinite.

At this hour of the morning, a very little of it went a long way with Michael Chivers. Hastitly, he turned away from it and headed for the hired car.

The sweet ted and toast hadn't set at all well with him. He needed something to settle his stomach, and he could think of only one thing that would do it. A bottle of good lager, or, better still, brown or summer ale. And he knew it was not to be found, so early in the day, in a community like Lacona beach. The bars here, the cocktail lounges, rather, would not open until shortly after midday. If there were morning drinkers in the town, and doubtless there were, they had their own private bars to drink from.

Turning the car toward the rental company, Michael drove out of the southerly outskirts of Lacuna beach and into the more quiet districts beyond, slowing occasionally for a swift gauging of the various drinking establishments. Many of them were open, but they were not the right kind. They would have only the East Coast beers, which, to Michael's way of thinking, were undrinkable. None of them, certainly, would have a good brown ale.

Nearing the rental car company, he drove on for a mile or so; then, swinging up a long slope, he entered a small town. There, after some fifteen minutes of wandering about, he found what he was looking for. It wasn't a fancy place at all; not one of those glossy cocktail lounges where drinks were secondary to atmosphere. Just a good well grounded looking bar, with an air that immediately inspired confidence.

The landlord was counting cash into his cash register when Michael entered. A graying, rawbone-looking man, with a bronzed wrinkled face, he nodded a greeting in the back-bar mirror. 'Yes, mister, what'll it be?'

Michael put a name to it, and the landlord said that certainly he had good ale: if ale wasn't good it was slop. 'Give you summer or brown.' Michael chose Brown ale, and the landlord was pleased at his gratified reaction.

'Good, huh? Y'know, I think I'll just have one myself.'

Michael took an immediate liking to the fella, and the feeling was reciprocated. He liked the look of this place, its unassuming honesty and good taste; the quiet pride of its owner in being its owner.

Within fifteen minutes they were on a first-name basis. Michael was explaining his presence in town, using his holidaying as an excuse for his own time drinking. Joe the landlord confessed that he also shunned the early morning drink; but he was going on vacation the following day, so what was the harm, anyway?

Two men came in, downed a double-shot rum each, and hurried out again. Joe looked after them with a touch of sadness, and came back to Michael. That was no way to drink, he said. Every so often, even the best of men need a drink or two in the morning, but they shouldn't drink it that way.

As he left to wait on another customer, he brushed against a back-bar display stand of crisps and salted nuts, moving it slightly out of its original position. And staring absently in that direction, Michael saw something that made him scowl. He stood up a little from his stool for another look, making sure of what he had seen. He sat down again, puzzled and troubled.

A punch board! A punch board in a place like this! Joe was no fool, either in the con or the everyday sense, but a punch board was strictly a deceiver's item.

Back at the time Michael was just starting out, there were still a few teams working the boards, one man planting them, the other knocking them over. But he hadn't seen any in years. Everyone had barbed long ago, and trying to plant a board now was the equivalent of asking for a busted jaw.

Of course, some small vendors, wholesalers, and barkeeps still bought boards on their own, punching out the winning numbers at the start and thus giving the suckers no chance at all. But Joe wouldn't do that. Joe

Michael laughed mockingly to himself, took a foamy sip of the ale. What was this, anyway? Was he, Michael Chivers, actually concerned about the honesty or dishonesty of a barkeep or the possibility that he might be swindled?

Another customer had come in, looking and dressed like a farm workman, and Joe was serving him a bottle of non-alcohol budweiser. Coming back down the bar with two fresh bottles of ale, he refilled their glasses. And Michael allowed himself to 'observe' the board.

'Oh, that board.' The landlord retrieved it from the back-bar and laid it in front of him. 'Some fellow walked out and left it almost a year ago. Didn't detect it until after he was gone. I was going to throw it away, but I get a customer now and then who wants to try his luck. So----' He paused tentatively. 'Want to have a try? Chances run from a hundred dollars minimum.'

'Well' Michael looked down at the board.

Attached to the top were several gold imitation bars, representing cash prizes of thousand to ten thousand dollars. Under each of them a number was printed. To win, one had only to punch out a corresponding number or numbers from the thousands on the board.

None of the winners had been punched out. Joe, evidently, was as honest as he looked.

'Well,' said Michael, picking up the little metal key which dangled from the board, 'what can I lose?'

He punched a few numbers, laying them out for Joe's inspection. On his fourth punch, he hit the six thousand dollar prize, and the landlord smilingly laid the money on the counter. Michael let it lay, again cool-headed the key over the board.

He couldn't tell Joe that this was a fall guy's stunt. To do so would let out knowledge that no honest man should have. Most certainly, and even though someone else was bound to do it, he couldn't take the man himself. The scamming just wasn't for him today, or so he defended. There just wasn't enough at stake.

If he knocked off every prize on the board, the take would be over ten thousand dollars. And naturally he'd never get away with knocking them all off. The big-league racket had always gone for the big one and left the others alone. He, however, had already hit the seven.

He punched out the eight thousand number. Still smiling, pleased rather than discomfit, Joe again laid money on the counter. Michael brought the key up for another punch.

This was the way to do it, he'd decided. The way to get the board out of circulation. One more prize was the main one, ten thousand and he'd point out that something must be weird about the board. Joe would be left with no option but to get rid of it. And he, of course, would refuse to accept his winnings.

He punched out another 'lucky' number. Properly surprised, he cleared his throat for the tip-off. But Joe, his smile slightly stiffened now, had turned to glance at the no-alcohol budweiser customer.

'Yes, mister?' he said. 'Something else?'

'Yes, Joe,' the man said, his voice menacingly light. 'Yes, Joe, there's something else, all right. You got a government gambling-tax stamp?'

'Huh! What---'

'Don't have one, eh? Well, I'll tell you something else you don't have; won't have it long, anyway. Your liquor license.'

'B--but---' Joe had faded under his tan. The parish liquor licenses were worth a tiny fortune. 'But you can't do that! We were just---'

'Tell it to the parish councillors and government boys. I'm local.' He flipped open a leather warrant-case; nodded coldly at Michael. 'You're pretty dopey, young man. No one but a pudding head would knock a fall guy off for several balls in a row.'

Michael looked at him evenly. 'I don't know what you're talking about,' he said. 'And I don't like your language.'

'On your feet! I'm arresting you for defrauding!'

'You're making a mistake, officer. I'm a salesman, and I---'

'Are you giving me a hard time? eh? Why, you scamming son-of-a-bitch!'

He grabbed Michael by the front of his jacket, pulled him violently to his feet and slammed him up against the wall.

Chapter 21

First, there was the search; the turning out of pockets, the checking and tapping of garments, the hand brought up on either side of the testicles. Then came the questions, the demanded answers that were immediately labeled lies.

'Your full name, goddamn you! Never mind those bogus credentials! All your cheaters got them!'

'That is my right name. I live in Castries, and I've worked for the same company for years--'

'Stop lying! Who's working the boards with you? How many other places have you pulled this trick?'

'My health has been bad. I came down to Laguna beach yesterday evening. A friend and I are on a holiday.'

'All right, all right! Now, we're going to start all over again and, by God, you better come clean! _'

'Officer, there are at least a half a century of businessmen here in town who can identify me. I've been selling to them for years, and---'

'_Drop it! Drop that dirt! Now, what's your full name!'

The same questions over and over. The same answers over and over. Now and then, the law enforcement officer turned to the walk radio to pass his information on for checking. But still, the information checking out, he would not give up. He knew what he knew. With his own eyes, he had seen the scammer work, a punch board rapidly knocked for several prizes. And Michael's perfect front notwithstanding, how could the clear evidence of defrauding be ignored?

He was on the radio again now, his heavy face swelled up as he got the answers to his questions. Michael sidled a glance at Joe the bar owner. He looked at the punchboard on the counter fixedly and again raised his eyes to Joe. Nodded to him ever so slightly. But he couldn't be sure that Joe got the message.

The law enforcement officer slammed up the radio. He stared at Michael bitterly, rubbed a meaty hand over his face. Pausing, he tried to form the words which the situation called for, the apology which outraged aptitude and defy the evidence of his own eyes.

From up the bar, Michael heard a slow grinding sound, the garbage disposal.

He smiled quietly to himself. 'Well, officer,' he said. 'Any more questions?'

'That's all.' The cop pulled his head. 'Looks like I may have made a mistake.'

'Yes? You clap me around and offend me and treat me like a criminal. And then you say you may have made a mistake. That's supposed to polish everything over.'

'Well---' mouth tight, choking over the words. 'Sorry. My apology. No offense.'

Michael was content to settle for that. Viciously, the cop turned on Joe.

'Okay, mister! I want the number of your liquor license! I'm turning you in for--for---Where's that punch board? _'

'What punch board?'

'Cripes you, don't you pull that dirt on me! The board that was right there on the counter---the one that this man was playing! Now, you either hand it over or I'll find it myself!'

Joe picked up a cloth and began mopping the counter. 'I normally clean up this time of day,' he said. 'Clear up all the odds and ends of discarded things and throw them down the garbage disposal. Now, I can't say that I recall any punch board, but if there was one here.'

'You threw it away! Y-you think you can get away with that?'

'Can't I?' Joe said.

The cop stuttered in furious illogic. He said, 'You'll see, on my time in the force, you'll see!' And turning savagely to Michael, 'You too, young man! You ain't got me tricked a damned bit! I'm going to be on the lookout for you, and the next time you hit this town!'

He turned and walked out of the place. Smiling, Michael sat back down at his stool.

'Acts like he's hurt about something,' he said. 'How about another ale?'

'No,' Joe said.

'What? Now, look, Joe. I'm sorry if there were any problems, but it was your punch board. I didn't---'

'I know. It was my fault. But I never make the same mistake more than once. Now, I want you to leave, and I don't want you to come back.'

Another customer came in, and Joe began to wait on him. Michael arose and walked out.

The striking sunlight struck against his face, its strength doubled with the contrast of the cool and shadowed bar. The cold brown ale, how much had he drunk, anyway? Enraged in his stomach, then uneasily settled back. He wasn't drunk, by any means. He never got drunk. But it wasn't smart to start back to Laguna beach without eating.

There was a small restaurant two streets down from where Joe's bar is, and he had a bowl of healthy chicken soup there and a cup of sweet tea. Startled, he noticed the time as he left, just a few minutes after midday, and he stared at his mobile. But he decided on calling Emily; so, he went on out to his car.

It was probably best not to call Emily, he decided. The law enforcement officer would have called her, and he didn't want to make explanations over the phone.

He went back down the long hill to the hotel, then took the road right toward the coast. It was about a fifteen minute's drive to the hotel he and Emily were holidaying in, fifteen minutes outside. Then, he would be back at the hotel with Emily, lightly explaining the law enforcement officer trouble as a---

A case of unwarranted identity? No, no. Something simpler, something that might logically evolve from an innocent circumstance. This car, for example, was a hired car. The last driver might have been involved in a serious traffic violation; he had fled, say, from the scene of an accident. So, when the law enforcement officer spotted the car this morning.

Well, sure, there were variations in the story: the law enforcement officer would have known it was a hired car by the license number. But that wasn't up to him to explain. He'd been the victim of a cop mistake; who could figure out their misinterpretation?

A hell of a morning, Michael thought. It was Joe's punch board. Why should he get tough with me? What the mother fuck do I care what a barkeep thinks?

Near the intersection with Highway seven, the traffic about him piled up and at the Highway itself it was stalled in a three-ane tangle which two law enforcement officers were struggling to undo. That didn't taunt the normal pattern of the day in this coastal town.

The cars move forward slowly, Michael's car moving with them. Almost a half-hour later, near Laguna Beach, he turned off the highway and into a service station. And here he learned the reason for the congestion.

The carnival floats, just a few were running at low speed. It was the local festival season in a week's time.

In another twenty minutes, the traffic had thinned, and rejoining it, he reached the hotel some ten minutes later. So, he was very late and entering the hotel he called Emily's room from the lobby. There was no answer, but she had left a message for him at the reception.

'Why, yes, Mr. Chivers. She said to tell you she'd gone to the cart-racing track.'

'The cart-racing?' Michael moaned. 'Are you sure?'

'Yes, Mr Chivers. But she was only going to stay for part of the day's program. She'll be back early, she said.'

'I see,' Michael nodded. 'By the way, was there a call from the cops about me a couple of hours ago?'

The reception admitted cautiously that there had been, also disclosing that there had been a similar call to Mrs. Emily Casey. 'Naturally, we spoke of you in the highest terms, Mr. Chivers.It was nothing serious, I hope?'

'Nothing, thanks,' Michael said, and he went on up to his room.

He stood for some time before the windows, staring out at the sun-sparkled sea. Then, eyes paining a little, he stretched out on the bed, letting his thoughts roam at will; piercing them together with notion and instinct until they formed a motive.

First there was her interest in the way he lived, the job he held. Why did he stay on, year after year, at a place like the Park Royal? Why did he hold on to, year after year, a relatively small-time commission job? Then, there were her sly complaints about their relationship: they didn't really know each other; they needed to 'get acquainted.' So, he had arranged this tour, a means of getting acquainted, and how did she use the time? Why, by putting him on his own, at every opportunity. And then sitting back to see what happened. He successfully robbed millions of dollars a few nights ago.

So now she knows; she must know. Her actions today proved that she did.

The cop had called her about him, yet she had not been disturbed. She had known that he would be all right, that just as his front had held up for years, it would continue to hold up in this trouble whatever that trouble was. So, having found out all that she needed to, she had gone off to the cart-races.

Suddenly, he sat up pulling a face, his mild annoyance with her turning to anger.

She had stalled on coming to Laguna beach hotel. After being so anxious for the trip, she had unreasonably found reason to postpone it, until this week.

Because this was the beginning of the carnivals. And the cart-racing tracks in the Castries area were temporarily inactive.

Or maybe not. He couldn't be sure that she was nosing into his sister Jasmine's business as she had nosed into his. It might be that she was simply angry at him for leaving her alone for so long, and that she had gone to the cart-races as a way of expressing her unhappiness.

Emily returned to the hotel around five o'clock. Feeling uneasy humorously over the discomforts of her taxi ride; pretending to look petulant at Michael for going off without her.

'I just thought I'd teach you a lesson, you big git! You're not angry, are you?'

'I'm not sure. I understand that the cops called you about me.'

'Oh, that,' she snatched. 'What was the problem, anyway?'

'You wouldn't have any idea?'

'Well----' She began to draw a little bit. Coming over to the bed, she sat down gingerly at his side. 'Michael, I've been wanting to talk to you for a long time. But before I could, I wanted to make sure that---'

'Let it ride a bit,' he said carelessly. 'Did you try to contact my sister Jasmine today?'

'Jasmine? Oh, you mean your sister. Isn't she the close friend of nurse Layla now?'

Michael said that she was. 'But Layla is angry with her work hours. Anyways Jasmine got business contacts at the kart-racing tracks in this parish. So, she could be down here, wouldn't she?'

'How do I know? What are you getting at, anyway?'

She started to get up. He held her, taking a grip on the front of her dress.

'Now, I'll ask you again. Did you see or try to contact my sister while you were out at the Kart-racing track?'

'No! How could I? I was in the grandstand!'

Michael smiled narrowly, pointing out her error. 'And Jasmine wouldn't be in the grandstand, hmm? Now how did you know that?'

'Because I--I--' She colored blamable. 'Okay, Michael, I saw her. I was meddling. But it's not like you think! I was just curious about her, wondering why she'd come to Laguna beach. And she was always so horrible to me! I knew she was striking me to you every chance she got. So I just thought who is she to be so high and mighty, and I talked with a friend of mine in Castries and--and---'

'I see. You must have some very knowledgeable friends.'

'Michael,' she begged. 'Don't be furious with me. I wouldn't do anything to hurt her any more than I would you.'

'You'd better never try,' he said. 'Jasmine travels in some very ruthless quick company.'

'I know,' she nodded delicately. 'I'm sorry, honey.'

'Jasmine didn't see you today?'

'Oh, no. I didn't hang around, Michael. Honest.' She kissed him, smiling into his eyes. 'Now, about us.'

'Yes,' he nodded. "We may as well go back to Castries, won't we? You've found out what you wanted to know.'

'Now, honey. Don't take it like that. I think I must have known for a longtime. I was just waiting for the right opportunity to talk to you.'

'And just what do you know about me, anyway?'

'I know you're a robber, short-con operator. A very good one, by all accounts.'

'You talk the patter. What's your pitch?'

'The twinkling of an eye robbery. The big con.'

He nodded; paused. She snuggled close to him, pressing his hand against her breast. 'We'd make a hell of a team, Michael. We think alike; we get along well together. Why, honey, we could work for three months out of the year, to cover our tracks and live high for the other nine! I---'

'Wait,' he said, gently pushing her away. 'This isn't something to rush into, Emily. It's going to take a lot of talking.'

'Well? So let's talk.'

'Not here. We didn't come here on business. We don't talk about it here.'

She searched his face, and her smile dimed a little. 'I see,' she said. 'You think it might be hard to give me a turndown here. It would be easier on the home grounds.'

'You're clever,' he said. 'Maybe you're too clever, Emily. But I didn't say I was turning it down.'

'Well---.' She shrugged and stood up. 'If that's the way you want it.'

'That's the way I want it,' he said.

Chapter 22

They caught the seven o'clock stagecoach back to Castries. It was crowded, as the stagecoach coming down had been, but the make-up of the crowd was different. These passengers were largely businesspeople, men who had put in a long day in their area of respectful jobs, and were now returning to their Castries homes, or those who lived close by and were due in Castries early in the morning. Then, there were those few who had overstayed their time, and faced reproaches, or worse, when they arrived in the city area.

The holiday feel was absent. A kind of gloominess pervaded the stagecoach, and some of it enveloped Emily and Michael.

They had a drink in the lounge. Then, discovering that the stagecoach carried no hot meals, or hot snacks, they remained in their seats for the rest of their ride. Seated in the cozy closeness of a window seat, her thigh pressed warmly against Michael's, Emily looked out at the aching loneliness of the sea, the naked and hungry hills, the large and small houses closed steadfastly to all but themselves. The point that she had put forward to him, something that was entirely desired, became a tigerish must---a thing that had to be. It was either that or nothing, and so it had to be that.

She could not go on as she had the past few years, attaining her capital with her body, exchanging her body's use for the sustenance it needed. There were not enough years left, and the body inevitably used more than it received. Always, as the years grew fewer, the more quickly the flesh drained itself. So, an end to things as they had been.

An end to the race with self. The mind grew youthful with use, increasingly eager with the demands of its owner, anxious and able to provide for the body that gave it shelter, to imbue it with its own youth and vigor or a reasonable facsimile thereof. And thus, the mind must be used from now on. The ever-lucrative projects which the mind could assemble and put into practice. Her mind and Michael's, the two working together as one, and the money which he could and must supply.

Perhaps she had pushed her hand a little too hard; no man liked to be pushed. Perhaps her interest in Jasmine Chivers had been a blunder; every man was sensitive about his sister. But it doesn't matter. What she suggested was right and reasonable. It would be good for both.

It was what had to be. And damn him, he'd better!

He made some casygoing comments, elbowing her for feedback, and seething with her own thoughts she turned on him, her face aged with anger. Alarmed, he drew back smirking.

'Hey, now! What's the matter?'

'Nothing. Just thinking about something.' She smiled, dropping the mask so quickly that he was not sure of what he had seen. 'What was it you said?'

He shook his head; he couldn't remember what it was now. 'But maybe I should know your name, woman. The right one.'

'How about Casey?'

'Casey----' He baffled over it for a bit. Then, 'Casey! You mean, The contractor? You teamed with him Casey?'

213

'That's me, buddy.'

'Well, now,' He paused. 'What happened to him, anyway? I heard a lot of stories, but ...

'The same thing that happens to all of them, a lot of them I mean. He just blew up; booze, marijuana, the lot.'

'I see,' he said. 'I see.'

'Now, don't you brood about him.' She curled up closer to him, misreading his attitude. 'That's all over and done with. There's just us now, Emily Casey and Michael Chivers.'

'He's still alive, isn't he?'

'Possibly. I really don't know,' she said.

And she might have said, And I don't care. For the knowledge had come to her immediately, though unsurprisingly, that she didn't care, that she had never really cared about him. It was as though she had been mesmerized by him, overwhelmed by his personality as others had been; forced to go his way, to accept his as the right and only way. Yet always intuitively resisting and resisting, slowly building up revulsion for being forced into a life, and what kind of life was it, anyway, for an attractive young woman? that was entirely foreign to the one she wanted.

It was nothing clear, defined. Nothing she was consciously aware of or could confess to. But still she knew, in her secret mind, knew and felt guilty about it. And so, when the blowup came, she tried to take care of him. But even that had been a means of hitting back at him, the final firm push over the brink and intuitively knowing this she had felt still more guilty and was cursed by him. Yet now, her feelings brought to the surface, she saw there was not and had never been anything to feel guilty about.

The contractor had got what he deserved. Anyone who cheated her out of something she wanted deserved what he got.

It was nine-thirty when the stagecoach pulled into Castries. She and Michael had a good dinner in the station restaurant. Then they ran through a light mist to his car and drove out to her apartment.

She threw off her jacket with great speed, turned to him, holding out her arms. He held her for a moment, kissing her, but inwardly drawing back a little, gingerly cautioned by something in her manner.

'Now,' she said, drawing him down onto the lounge, 'Now, we get down to business.'

'Do we?' He laughed clumsily. 'Before we do that, maybe we'd better--'

'I can scrape up two and a half million without much trouble. That would leave one million for your end. There's a place in Rodney Bay now, wide open if the ice is right. As good as Cape Marquis was in the old days. We can move in there with a wire store, and---'

'Wait,' said Michael. 'Hold it!'

'It would be perfect, Michael! Say, one million for the store, and another one million for---'

'I said to hold it! Not so fast,' he said, raging a little now. 'I haven't said I was going to throw in with you.'

'What?' She looked at him absently, a modest stare over her eyes. 'What did you say?'

He repeated the words, softening it with a laugh. 'You're talking about some tall figures. What makes you think I've got that kind of money?'

'Why, you must have! You're bound to!' She smiled at him strongly; an adult reprimanded a rude youngster. 'Now, you know you do, Michael.'

'Do I?'

'Yes. I watched you work on the stagecoach, as slick an operator as I ever saw. You don't get that smooth overnight. It takes years, and you've been getting away with it for years. Living as a law-abiding citizen and taking the fools for---'

'And I've been doing some taking myself. Twice in less than a month. Enough to put me in the health Centre here.'

'So what?' She brushed the intervention aside. 'That doesn't change anything. All it proves is that it's time you moved up. Get up where there's big dough at stake and you don't have to be lucky every day and get about every day.'

'Maybe I like it where I am.'

'Well, I don't like it! What are you trying to pull on me, anyway? What the hell are you trying to hand me?'

He stared at her, not knowing whether to laugh or be angry, his lips pursing distrustfully. He had never seen this woman before. He had never heard her before.

The mist covered the window. Distantly, there was a faint droning of an elevator. And with it, with those sounds, the sound of her heavy wheezing. Labored, angry.

'I'd better dash along now,' he said. 'We'll talk about it some other time.'

'We'll talk about it now, my Gosh!'

'Then,' he said quietly, 'there's nothing to talk about, Emily. The answer is no.'

He stood up. She jumped up with him.

'Why?' she commanded. 'Just tell me why, damn you!'

Michael nodded, a gleam coming into his eyes. He said that the best reason he could think of was that she frightened the hell out of him. 'I've met people like you before, girl. Double-tough and piercing as a staple, and they get what they want or else. But they won't get by with it forever.'

'Nonsense!'

'You know this, history. Sooner or later the fire burns them, girl. I don't want to be around when it burns you.'

He started for the door. Wild-eyed, her face colorized with fury, she flung herself in front of him.

'It's your sister, isn't it? Sure, it is! One of those keeps the money in the family deals! That's why you act so weird around each other! That's why you were living in her apartment!'

'What?' He came to a full stop. 'What are you saying?'

'Don't act so goddamned crimeless! You and your own sister, gah! I'm wise to you, I should have seen it before! Why, you evil mother fucker! How is it, hmm? How do you like--'

'How do you like this?' Michael said.

He slapped her in the spur of the moment, catching her with a backhanded slap as she wobbled. She leaped at him, hands clawed, and he grabbed her by the hair and flung her, and she came down stretch out on the floor.

A little wonderingly he looked at her, as she raised her blotched and reddened face. 'You see?' he said. 'You see why it wouldn't do, Emily?'

'You d-dirty bastard! You're going to see something!'

'I'm sorry, Emily,' he said. 'Good night and good luck?'

Chapter 23

At the corner outside her apartment house, he waited around briefly before entering his car; relishing the mist against his face, liking the cool, clean feel of it. Here was normality, something atmospheric and honest. He was very happy he was out here in the mist instead of up there with her.

Back at the Park Royal, he lay awake for a time, thinking about Emily; wondering at how little sense of loss he felt at losing her.

Was tonight purely a finalizing of something that he had long intended to do? It seemed so; it had the feeling about it of the expected. It might even be that his strong attraction for Layla had been a reaction to Emily, an attempt to attach himself to another woman and consequently be detached from her.

Layla----

He fidgeted agonizingly, then put her out of his mind. He'd have to do something about her, he decided. Sometime soon, somehow, he'd have to smooth things over with her.

As for Emily----

He moaned, on the point of falling asleep, then relaxed with a shake of his head. No, no danger there. She'd gotten angry and blown her top, but she was probably regretting it already. At any rate, there was nothing she could do, and she was too smart to try. Her own position was too fragile. She was wide open for a smacking-down herself.

He fell into a deep sleep. Having slept so little the night before, he rested well. And it was after eight when he awakened.

He jumped out of bed, feeling good and full of energy, starting to plan the day's schedule as he reached for a robe. Then slowly, desolate, he sat back down. For here he was again as he had been last week. Here he was again, still, confronted by emptiness. Against the law from his selling job, against the law from any activity. Faced with a day, an endless series of days, with nothing to do.

Listlessly, he cursed Mr. Senior.

He cursed himself.

Again, hopefully hopeless, as he showered and shaved, as he dressed and went out to breakfast, he sought some way out of the stalemate. He needed to invest the one and a half million banknotes he robbed, but how and where? He needed time before he could start investing that money, because it would look too suspicious. And his mind came up with the same answers, answers which were wholly unacceptable.

One: He could take the sales manager's job, take it without further stalling around, and give up the scamming. Or, two: He could leave Castries and go to another city; begin all over again as he had begun when he first left his sister's house at the age of eighteen.

Breakfast over, he got into his car and began to drive, pointlessly, without destination; the most exhausting way of driving. When this became unbearable, as it very shortly did, he pulled into the side street and parked.

irritably, his mind returned to the infeasible problem.

Senior, he thought angrily. That damned Senior. Why couldn't he have left me alone? Why did he have to be so damned sure that I---

The vain thinking interrupted itself. His frown grew dim, and a slow smile played around his lips.

Senior was a man of click judgment, a man who made up his mind in a hurry. So probably he would unmake it just as fast. He would take no nonsense from anyone. Given ample reason, and without apology, he would snatch back from the sales manager's job as promptly as he had recommended.

Michael called him. He was still forbidden to work for a while (the doctor's orders), he said, but perhaps Senior would like to have lunch with him? Senior said that he seldom took time for lunch; he usually settled for noodles, or sandwiches in his office.

'Maybe you should start going out,' Michael told him.

'Oh? You mean on account of my ulcers?'

'I mean on account of your temperament. It might help you to get along better with people.'

He smirked coldly, listening to the spooked silence that poured over the wire. Then, Senior said equably, 'Well, maybe it would at that. One o'clock suits you?'

'No, it doesn't. I'd rather eat at twelve thirty.'

Senior said, fine, that was better for him, too. 'Twelve thirty then. The little place across the road.'

Michael hung up the phone. He considered the advisability of showing up late for the appointment and decided against it. That would be simply bad-mannered, harsh. It would do nothing but arouse Senior suspicions.

Already, perhaps, he had followed the line of abruptness too far.

He arrived at the restaurant a little after twelve. They ate at a small table in the rear of the dining area, and somehow the meeting went pretty much as the first one had. Somehow, and much to Michael's vexation, the feeling of empathy grew between them. Toward the end of the meal, Senior did an alarming thing---alarming, that is, for him. Reaching across the table, he gave Michael a timid knock on the arm.

'Feeling lazy, aren't you, young man? Like you could be in suspense.'

'What?' Michael looked at him shocked. 'What makes you think that?'

'You'd just have to; I know I would. A man can do nothing around so long, and then it begins to drive him crazy. Why don't you come back to the office with me for a while? Sort of look the setup over.'

'Well, I---you're busy, and---'

'So I'll put you to work, too.' Senior stood up, smiling. 'I'm joking, of course. You can just look around; peek at the salesmen's file, if you like. Do what you want to and pull out when you want to.'

'Well,' Michael brushed aside. 'Why not?'

The question was linguistic; he could think of no valid reason to turn down the chance. Similarly, finding himself in Mr. Senior's office at the huge main store, he was forced to accept the file which Senior pushed in front of him. To show at least a pretence of interest in its various file papers.

Bitterly, he saw himself a victim of Senior domineeringness. Senior had taken charge of him again, as he had on that first day. But that wasn't true. More precisely, he was his own victim, his own mental slave. He had made personality a profession, created a career out of selling fake products. And he could not wander off far, or for long, from his self-made self.

He looked through the sheets of paper, unseeing.

He began to see them, to read the meaning in them. They became people and money and life itself. And thoughtfully, one at a time, he took them out of the file and spread them out on the desk.

He picked up a yellow highlighter, reached for a lined pad of scratch paper.

As he worked, Senior gave him an occasional disguise peep, and a pleasing smile tightened his thin lips. A couple of hours passed, and Senior arose and walked over to his desk.

'How are you getting on?'

'Sit down,' Michael said, and as the other man obeyed, 'I think this record system is all wrong, Mr. Senior. I don't want to tread on anyone's toes, whoever set it up, but---'

'Tell me more. Nothing's angelic around here.'

'Well, it's misleading, a waste of time. Take this person here. His gross sales for the week are fifty-five thousand dollars. His commission, over in this column, totals eighty-one thousand dollars. What's his percentage of the week's sales?'

'I'd have to figure it up. Roughly, a decent percent.'

'Not necessarily. Depending on what he sold, he might have some enough per cent stuff in there. The point is, just what the hell was it that he sold? How much of it was practically loss-leader stuff, items that we have to sell to compete?'

Senior looked at him sharply; paused. 'Well, of course, there's his sales slips; that's what his commissions were figured from.'

'But where are the sales slips?'

'Accounting gets a copy, inventory gets a copy, and of course the customer gets one at the time of purchase.'

'Why does inventory need a copy? The stuff is checked off at the time it leaves the shop, isn't it? Or at least it could be. You've got some duplicate effort if it isn't. Where you need a copy is here in the salesman's file.'

'But---'

'Not in a file like this, of course. There isn't enough room. But it docsn't have to be like this. We don't have so many salesmen that we set up a separate file on each one on a spreadsheet, giving each man a section in one of the files online.'

Mr. Senior scratched his head. 'Hmm,' he said. 'Well maybe.'

'It ought to be done, Senior. It just about has to be if you're going to have a clear picture of what's going on. Tie the sales slips to the salesmen, and you know which men are selling and which are running a milk route. Doing one's bidding. You know what items are moving and which need pushing, and which should be dropped entirely. Of course, you'll know all that eventually, anyway. But waiting can cost you a hell of a lot of money and-'

Michael broke off unexpectedly, suddenly abashed by his tone and his words. He shook his head, dismayed, like a man coming into alertness.

'Just listen to me,' he said. 'I come in here for the first time, and I start kicking your structure to pieces.'

'So straighten it some more. Straighten the crap out of it!' Senior beamed at him. 'How are you feeling, anyway? Getting tired? Want to knock off for the day?'

'No, I'm okay. But---'

'Well, let's see, then.' Senior skidded his chair closer and reached for a highlighter. 'What would you say to----.'

Half an hour went by.

Onehours.

In the outer offices, one of the receptions turned a shocked look on her neighbor. 'Did you hear that?' she whispered. 'He was laughing! Old gloomy Senior laughed out loud!'

'I heard,' said the other girl, seriously, 'but I don't believe it. That guy never learned how to laugh!'

At four-thirty that afternoon, the telephone operator plugged in her night numbers and closed her board. The outer offices darkened and became silent, as the last of the office works clocked out. And at five, the ground floor staff departing to the muted chiming of the time-clock, the silence and the blurriness became full.

At eight o'clock--

Mr. J. Senior rubbed his eyes. He looked around, winking distractedly, and a baffled look spread over his face. With a flabbergasted evil eye, he jumped to his feet.

'Oh my gosh! Look at the time! Where the hell did the day go?'

'What?' Michael moaned. 'What's the matter, Senior?'

'Come on, you're getting out of here! Right this minute, for goodness sake! My God---' Senior swore again. 'I ask you to drop in for a few minutes and you put in a day's work!'

They had a late dinner together.

As they said goodbye, Senior gave him a sharp searching glimpse. 'Be straight with me, Michael,' he said quietly. 'You do want this job, don't you? You want to be a sales manager?'

'Well---' Michael paused for a nano second.

There it was. Here was his chance to decline. And he knew there and then that he could decline, without apology or explanation. He could say simply no, that he didn't want it, and that would be that. He could go back to his old life of robbery, defrauding, where he had left it. For something had happened between him and Senior, something that made them friends. And friends do not question each other's motives.

'Why, of course, I want it,' he said sternly. 'What gave you the idea that I didn't?'

'Nothing. I just thought that---nothing.' Senior returned to his usual smartness. 'I'm done with it. I'm done with you for the night. Go home and get some sleep, and don't show up at the store again until the doctor says you're ready!'

'You're the boss,' Michael smiled broadly. "Night, Senior.'

Driving back to the Park Royal, he started to justify his decision, to find some deceitful reason for doing what he had done. But that passed very swiftly. Why shouldn't he take a job that he wanted to take? Why shouldn't a man want a friend, a bona fide friend, when he has never before had one?

He put the car away and entered the Park Royal. The elderly night porter greeted him.

'You had a message this morning, Mr. Chivers. Your sister.'

'My sister?' Michael paused. 'Why didn't you leave a word for me where I work?'

'I was going to, sir, but she said not to bother. Didn't have time to hang on, I guess.'

Michael picked up his mobile phone, put in a call to Jasmine's. He hung up a minute or two later, confused, troubled.

Jasmine was gone. She had checked out of her house this morning, leaving no forwarding address, just the expensive furniture.

He went upstairs. moaning, he came out of his clothes and lay down on the bed. He twitched and turned for a while, worrying. Then, slowly, he relaxed and began to take a nap.

Jasmine could take care of herself. There could be---must be an innocent reason for her unexpected move.

Gros Islet. She might have moved there for some big money scam. Or she might have found a more desirable villa to purchase here in town that had to be taken immediately. Or perhaps Ethan Riley had suddenly recalled her to Dennery.

He fell asleep.

After what seemed only a short time, he came awake.

Sunlight flooded the room. It was late in the morning. He was aware that the mobile phone had been ringing for a very long time. It was now silent, but the phone ringtone was still in his ears. He started to reach for it, his senses sluggish, not fully free of the daze of sleep, and there was a knock on the door, a persistent knocking.

He crossed to it, opened it enough to look out. He glinted at the man there; then, the man identified himself, declaring his business with professional remorse, apologizing for the journey that had brought him here. Michael let the door open wide.

And he stood shaking his head as the man came inside.

No, he shouted silently. It can't be true! It was some stupid mistake! Jasmine wouldn't be in Dennery! Why---why--

He said it aloud, staring at his visitor. The visitor pursed his lips thoughtfully.

'You didn't know she was in Dennery, Mr. Chivers? She didn't tell you she was going?'

'Of course, she didn't! Because she didn't go! I--- I---' He paused, some of his alertness asserting itself. 'I mean, my sister and I weren't very close. We went our own ways. I hadn't seen her for almost four years until she came here just over a month ago, but----'

'I understand,' the man nodded. 'That scoff with our information, such as it is.'

'Well, you're wrong, anyway,' Michael said doggedly. 'It's someone else. My sister wouldn't---'

'I'm afraid not, Mr. Chivers. It was her own gun, registered to her. The owner of the tourist villas remembers that she was very beside herself. Of course, it does seem a little odd that she'd use a gun with a silencer on it for---for something like that. But---'

'And she didn't! It doesn't make sense!'

'It never does, Mr. Chivers. It never makes sense when a person takes their own life

Chapter 24

The man was somewhat finely dressed, heavy-set, with a round, orange face. His name was Dennis, and he was a Treasury Department agent. Obviously, he felt a little awkward about being here at such a time. But it was his job, unpleasant though it might be, and he meant to do it. He did, however, lead into his business twistingly.

'You understand why I came rather than the local family liaison cop, Mr. Chivers. It really isn't their affair, at least at this point. I'm afraid there may be some horrible publicity later on, when the circumstances of your sister's death are disclosed. An attractive young lady with so much money in her possession. But---'

'I see,' said Michael. 'The hard cash.'

'More than a million dollars, Mr. Chivers. Hidden in the trunk of her car. And another one point five million found in her villa apartment. I'm very much afraid--' softly. 'I'm afraid she hadn't paid taxes on it. She'd been falsifying her returns for years.'

Michael gave him a disgusted look. 'The body was discovered this morning; about seven o'clock, right? You seem to have been a very busy man.'

Dennis agreed simply that he had been. 'Our office here hasn't had time to do a thorough research, but the evidence is incontestable. Your sister couldn't have saved that much out of her reported income. She was a tax evader.'

'How awful! Too bad you can't put her in jail.'

'Please!' Dennis drew back. 'I know how you feel.'

'I'm sorry,' Michael said quietly. 'That wasn't very fair. Just what do you want me to do, Mister. ?'

'Well--- I'm required to ask if you mean to lay claim to the money. If you care to say, that is. Possibly you'd rather consult a lawyer before you decide.'

'No,' Michael said. 'I won't lay any application to the money. I don't need it, and I don't want it.'

'Thank you. Thank you very much. Now, I wonder if you can give me any intelligence as to the source of your sister's income. It seems apparent, you know, that there must have been tax evasions on the part of others.'

Michael shook his head. 'I imagine you know as much about my sister's associates as I do, Mister. Maybe,' he added, with an exhaustedly crooked smile, 'you know much more than you're letting on.'

Dennis nodded seriously, and stood up. Pausing, briefcase in hand, he peeped around the room. And there was acceptance in his eyes, and a quiet concern.

Jasmine's money had had to be taken possession of, he murmured; her car, everything she owned included the villa. But Michael mustn't think that the government was merciless in these matters. Any sum necessary for her funeral would be released.

'You'll want to see the arrangements personally, I imagine. But if there's anything I can do to help. ' He took a business card from his wallet and laid it on the table. 'If you can tell me when you might care to leave for Dennery, if you are going, that is, I'll inform the local authorities and---'

'I'd like to go now.Just as soon as I can get a ticket.'

'Let me help you,' Dennis said.

He picked up the mobile phone, and called the ticket office. He spoke quickly, reciting a government code number. He peeped at Michael. 'Get you out in two hours, Mr. Chivers. Or if that's too soon.'

'I'll make it. I'll be there,' Michael said, and he began throwing on his clothes.

Dennis accompanied him to his car, shook hands with him warmly as Michael opened the door.

'Good luck to you, Mr. Chivers. I Wish we could have met under better circumstances.'

'You've been fine,' Michael told him. 'And I'm pleased we met, regardless.'

He had never seen the traffic worse than it was that day. It took all his concentration to get through it, and he was glad for the rest from thinking about Jasmine. He got to the station with fifteen minutes to spare. Picking up his ticket, he hurried toward the gate to his train. And then, moved by a sudden feeling, he swerved into the mens toilets.

A minute later he loomed from it. Looking serious and, with a cold anger in his heart, he went onto his train.

It was a prop job since his trip was a relatively short one, As it circled the area and winged south-eastwards, a train stewardess began serving the lunches and drinks. Michael took a double vodka. Sipping it, he settled back in his seat and stared out the window. But the drink was tasteless and he gazed at nothing.

Jasmine. My precious Jasmine.

She hadn't dispatched herself. She'd been murdered.

For. Emily Casey was also gone from her apartment. Emily also had checked out last night, leaving no forwarding address.

There was one thing about playing the perspectives. If you played them long enough, you knew the other guy's as well as you knew your own. Most of the time it was like you were looking out the same mirror. Given a certain set of circumstances, you knew just about what he would do or what he had done.

So, without actually knowing what had happened, just how and why Jasmine had been brought to her death, Michael knew enough. He could make a guess which came amazingly close to the truth.

Emily had a contact in Dennery. Emily knew that Jasmine would be carrying a handgun, that, like any successful operator, she would have accumulated a substantial deal of money which would never be very far from her. As to just how far, just where it might be hidden, Emily didn't know. She might look forever without finding it. Thus Jasmine had had to be put on the run; for, running, she would take the loot with her, necessarily reducing its possible whereabouts to her immediate district.

How to make her run? No difficulties there. For a fearful gloom lies constantly over the residents of Fairfax Street. It casts itself through the presumingly friendly handshake, or the lovely wrapped package. It shines out from the children's schools, the flower and teddy bears shops, the beauty parlor. Every neighbor is suspect, every outsider, everyone period; even one's own husband or wife or lovers. There is no ease on Fairfax Street. The longer one's tenancy, the more untenable it becomes.

You didn't need to scare Jasmine. Only to scare her a bit more. And if you had a contact at her home base, someone to give her a 'friendly warning.'

Michael finished his drink.

He ate the salad which the stewardess served him.

She took the tray away and he smoked a cigarette, and the train slowed closer over the overhead bridge and came into the Tram station in a creeping impression.

An unmarked law enforcement car was waiting for him at the station. It carried him rapidly into the district, and a law enforcement detective took him into a private office and gave him as much details as he could.

'Jasmine checked into the villa court around eleven last night, Mr. Chivers. It's that big place with several swimming pools; you passed it on the way into town. The night porter says she seemed pretty shaky, but I don't know that you can put much stock in that. People always remember that other people acted or looked or talked funny after something's happened to them. Anyway, your sister left a eighty-thirty call, and when she didn't answer her phone one of the housekeepers finally got around to looking in on her.'

Jasmine was dead. She was lying in bed in her pajamas. The gun was on the floor at the side of the bed. Judging by her appearance, Michael winced she'd put the muzzle at the jaw of her head and pulled the trigger.

There was no dishevelment in the room, no sign of a scuffle, no suicide note. 'That's about all we know, Mr. Chivers,' the detective concluded, and he added with casual calmness, 'Unless you can tell us anything.'

Michael said that he couldn't and that was a fact. He could only say what he suspected, and such guilty suspicions would only harm him while proving nothing at all against Emily. It might make a little trouble for her, cause her to be picked up and questioned, but it would achieve no more than that.

'I don't know what I could tell you,' he said. 'I've got an idea that she traveled with a pretty ruthless crowd, but I'm sure you're already aware of that.'

'Yes.'

'Do you think she might not have taken her life? That someone killed her?'

'No,' the detective scowed, reluctantly. 'I can't say that I think that. Not exactly. There's nothing to stipulate murder. It does seem odd that she'd come all the way from Castries to kill herself and that she'd get into her pajamas before doing it, but, well, taking one's own life does strange things. I'd say that she was badly startled, so petrified of being killed that she went out of her mind.'

'That sounds feasible,' Michael nodded. 'Do you think someone followed her to the villa? The person who'd startled her, I mean.'

'Possibly. But the villa court is close to the highway, you know. People are coming in and out at all hours. If the guilty person was one of them, it would be more or less impossible to tag him, and short of getting his confession to make a death threat, I don't know how we could stick him if he was flagged.'

Michael mumbled agreement. There was only one thing more that he could say, one more little nudge toward Emily that he could safely give the detective.

'I'm sure you've already looked into it, detective, but what about fingerprints or DNA? Wouldn't they, erm---'

'Fingerprints, DNA' the officer smiled sadly. 'DNA is for forensic stories, Mr. Chivers. If you dusted this office, you'd probably find twenty of smudged prints, and unless you knew when they were made and just who you were looking for, I don't know what the devil you'd do with them. Apart from that, criminals at work have an unfortunate habit of wearing gloves, and many of the worst ones have no police record. Your sister, for example, had never been attacked or printed. I'm sorry,' he added quickly. 'I didn't mean to refer to her as a criminal. But----'

'I understand,' Michael said. 'It's all good'

'Now, there are a few items of your sister's personal property which you'll want. Her necklace, diamond ring and so on. If you'll just sign this receipt.'

Michael signed, and was given a large brown envelope. He packed it in a bag, the sorrowful residue of Jasmine's hard and troubled years, and the detective escorted him back to the waiting unmarked law enforcement car.

The undertaking establishment was on a side road, a alleviating, eye-catching building of white decorative finish which blazed blindly in the afternoon sun. But inside it was almost shockingly cool. Michael trembled slightly as he stepped into the too amoral interior; the manager of the place, apparently notified of his coming, sprang forward sympathetically.

'So sorry, Mr. Chivers. So terribly sorry. No matter how we try to prepare for these fatal moments---'

'I'm fine.' Michael removed his arm from the man's grasp. 'I'd like to see my sister, please.'

'Shouldn't you sit down for a minute first? Or perhaps you'd like a weak tea.'

'No,' Michael said sternly. 'I wouldn't.'

'It might be best, Mr. Chivers. It would give us a little time to, uh---
-Well, you understand, sir. Due to the exceptional financial involvements, we have been unable to perform the beauty aids duties which we ordinarily would. The loved one's remains, the poor dear face.'

Snappily, Michael cut him off. He understood, he said. Also, he said, enjoying the manager's grimace of distaste, he knew what a bullet fired into a woman's jaw could do to her face.

'Now, I want to see her. Now!'

'As you wish, sir!' The man drew himself up. 'Please follow me!'

He led the way to a clean, shiny tiled room behind the chapel.

The cold here was icy. A series of drawers was set into one of the frostily gleaming walls. He gripped a drawer by its metal handle and gave it a tug, and it glided outward on its bearings. With an offended signal, he stepped back and Michael advanced to the crypt and looked into it.

He looked and looked quickly away.

He started to turn away. And then, slowly, hiding his surprise, he forced his eyes back on the woman in the box.

They were about the same size, the same coloring; they had the same full but beautifully
boned bodies. But the hands! The hand! Where was the evil burn that had been inflicted on it, where was the scar that such a burn must leave?

Well, doubtless it was on the hand of the woman who had killed this woman. The woman whom Emily Casey had intended to kill, and who had killed Emily Casey instead.

Chapter 25

It was late evening when the dirty car reached downtown Castries; pulled up a few doors short of the Park Royal. The driver leaned tediously over the wheel for a moment, hobbling with tiredness, a little giddy from sleeplessness. Then, resolutely, she raised her head, removed the tinted sunglasses, and studied herself in the mirror.

Her eyes were stiffened, bloodshot, but that didn't matter, They would probably be a hell of a lot worse, she suspected, before she was safely out of this mess. The glasses covered them, also helping to disguise her face. With the glasses on, and with the scarf drawn tightly around her head and under her chin, she could pass as Emily Casey. She'd done it back at the villa court in Dennery, and she could do it again.

She made some minor arrangements on the scarf, pulling it a bit lower on her forehead. Then, throwing off her weariness, subjecting it to her will, she got out of the car and entered the Park Royal.

The reception greeted her with the apprehensive smile of the aged. He heard her summons, a command, rather, and a touch of uncertainty suffused his smile.

'Well, er, Mr. Chivers out of town, Miss Casey Went to Dennery this morning, and---'

'I know that, but he's due back in just under thirty minutes, I'm supposed to meet him here. Now, if you'll kindly give me his key.

'But--but--wouldn't you like to wait down there?'

'No, I would not!' Domineeringly she held out her hand. 'The key, please!'

Scrambling around, he took the key from the rack and gave it to her. Looking after her, as she swung toward the stairs, he thought with non-bitterness that fear was the worst part of being old. The concern born of fear. A fella knew that he wasn't much upstanding any more, oh yes, he knew it. And he knew he didn't always talk too clever, and he couldn't really look nice no matter how hard he tried. So, knowing in his heart that it was impossible to please anyone, he scuffled in a fearless manner to please everyone. And thus he made mistakes, one after the other. Until, finally, he could no more bear himself than other people could bear him. And he passed away.

But maybe, he thought confidently, this would be fine. After all, Miss. Casey and Mr. Chivers were good friends. And visitors did sometimes wait in a guest's room when the guest was out.

Entering Michael's room, the woman locked the door and drooped against it, shortly resting. Then, dropping the sunglasses and her smartly large handbag on the bed, she went resolutely to the four box-framed comic entertaining pictures. They had caught her attention the first time she had seen them, something that struck a grate on note; entirely conflicting with the known tastes of their owner. They couldn't have been there as decoration, so they must serve another purpose. And without seeing the representing in the four wisely laughing faces; Michael Chivers, she had predicted what that purpose was.

Now, snooping loose the backs of the pictures, she saw that her guess was right.

The money tumbled out, sheaf after sheaf of currency. packing it into her bag, she was struck with unwilling affection for Michael; he must be good to have piled up this much. Then, stifling this emotion, telling herself that the theft would be good for him by pointing out the fruitlessness of crime, she finished her work by hand.

Large as it was, the bag bulged with its burden of loot. She could barely close the clip, and she wasn't at all sure that it would stay closed.

She lifted it up, moaning. She put it under her arm, covering an end of the stole over it, and looked at her appearance in the mirror. It didn't look bad, she thought. Not bad at all. If only the damned thing didn't fly open as she was passing through the reception area! She considered the advisability of leaving some of the money behind, and unexpectedly she decided to leave some. She needed half of the dough..

She gave the mirror a final swift peek. Then, her purse clutched tightly under her arm, she crossed to the door and unlocked it, pulled it open. And fell back with a startle puff.

'Hello, Jasmine,' said Michael Chivers.

Chapter 26

The basic details of her story were just about what Michael expected them to be.

First there had been the warning call from Dennery; then, responding to it, her frantic, unreasoning flight. She drove as hard as she could and as long as she could. When she could go no further, she turned in at the villa court.

The place had a service garage, rather than individual car ports, and she hadn't liked that. But she was too exhausted to go farther; and since a service garage attendant was on duty at all times, she could not reasonably object to the system.

She put the loaded gun under her pillow. She undressed and went to bed. Yes, as might be expected she had locked her door, but that probably didn't mean much. Those places, hotels and villa tourist courts, lost so many keys that they often had them made replaceable, the same master keys unlocking different doors. And that was surely the case here.

Anyway, she awakened hours later, with two hands clutching her throat. Hands that silenced any outcry she might make as they strangled her to death. She couldn't see who it was; she didn't care. She had been warned that she would be killed, and now she was being killed and that was enough to know.

She got the gun from under her pillow. Recklessly, she had shoved it upward, into the jaw of her attacker. And pulled the trigger.

Jasmine shuddered spasmodic, her voice breaking. 'Damn, Michael, you don 't know what it was like! What it means to execute someone! Allyour life you hear about it and read about it, but when you do it yourself.

Emily was in her pajamas, an old trick of nocturnal interlopers. Caught in another's room, they lay it to accident, claiming that they left their own room on some innocent mission and somehow got sidetracked into the wrong one.

There was a tagged key in Emily's pocket, the key to a nearby room. Also, it was the key to Jasmine's predicament. It pointed to a plan, ready-made, and without thinking she knew what she must do.

She put Emily in her bed. She wiped her own fingerprints from the gun, and pressed Emily's prints upon it. She spent the night in Emily's room, and in the morning she checked out under Emily's name and with the dead woman's clothes.

Naturally, she couldn't take her own car. The car and the money hidden in it now belonged to Emily also. Because Emily was now Jasmine Chivers, and Jasmine was Emily Casey. And so it must always be.

'What a mess! And all for nothing, I surmise. I was acceptable and excellent with Ethan all the time, but now that it's happened---' She paused, illuminating a bit. 'Well, maybe it's a break for me, after all. I've been wanting out of the malfeasance for years, and now I'm out. I can make a clean start, and---'

'You've already made a start,' Michael said. 'But it doesn't look very clean to me.'

'I'm sorry. ' Jasmine flushed culpable. 'I hated to take your money, but---'

'Don't be sorry, 'Michael said. 'You're not taking it.'

For a long moment, a silent twenty seconds eternity, Jasmine sat looking at her brother Staring into eyes that were her eyes, meeting a look as level as her own. So much alike, she thought, and the thought was also his. Why can 't I make him understand? she thought. And he thought, Why can't I make her understand?

Shiveringly, a cold deadness growing in her heart, she arose and went into the bathroom. She bathed her face in the face-sink, patted it dry with a towel, filled a small glass of water, and took a drink of it. Then, thoughtfully, she refilled the glass and carried it out to her brother. Why, thank you, leave it by the side table. Jasmine, he said, touched by the small respect. And Jasmine told herself, He's asking for it. I helped him when he was knocking on death's door, and if he tries to hold out on me now.

'I have to have that dough, Michael,' she said. 'She had a bankcard in her purse, but that doesn't do me any good. I can't risk blowing it. All she had on her was a few thousand bucks, and what the hell am I going to do with that?'

Michael said she could do quite a bit with it. A few thousand would get her to Praslin or some other distant parish. It would give her a month to live quietly while she looked for a job.

'A job!' Jasmine wheezed. 'I'm in my late twenties, and I've never held a legit job in my life!'

'You can do it,' Michael said. 'You're smart and attractive. There are any number of jobs you can hold. Just dump the scoundrel somewhere. Bury it. A trickster won't fit in with the way you'll be living, and---'

'Save it!' Jasmine cut him off with an angry, stabbing motion. 'You stand there telling me what to do, a man so crooked that he eats at restaurants!'

'I shouldn't have to tell you. You should be able to see it for yourself.' Michael inclining forward. 'A legit job and a quiet life are the only way for you, Jasmine. You start showing up at the tracks or the hot spots and Ethan's boys will be on you.'

'I know that,God dammit! I know I've gotta lay low, and I will.'

'It's good advice, Jasmine. I'm pursuing it myself.'

'Yeah, sure you are! I see you giving up the swindling!'

'What's so weird about it? It's what you wanted. You kept pushing it at me.'

'Okay,' Jasmine said. 'So you're on the level. So you don't need the money, do you? You don't need it or want it. So why the hell won't you give it to me?'

Michael sighed; tried to explain why: to explain acceptably the most difficult of suggestions; meaning, that the painful thing you are doing for a person is really for his or her own good. And yet, talking to her, watching her discomfort, there was in his mind, unadmitted, an almost callous rejoicing. Paying heed back to childhood, perhaps, rooted back there, back in the time when he had known need or desire, and been contradicted because the gainsay was good for him. Now it was his turn. Now he could do the right thing, and yes, it was right, simply by doing nothing. And so he must safeguard her. Keep her from the danger which the money would inevitably lead her to. Keep her available.

'Now, look, Jasmine,' he said sensibly. 'That money wouldn't last you forever; maybe eight or maximum ten years. What would you do then?'

'Well. I'd think of something. Don't worry about that part.'

Michael nodded evenly. 'Yes,' he said, 'you'd think of something. Another swindle. Another Ethan Riley to slap you around and burn holes in your hand. That's the way it would turn out, Jasmine; that way or worse. If you can't change now, while you're still relatively young, how could you do it when you were pushing near forty?'

Fifty? There was an old sound about it and the odor of terrible and the cowardly look of death.

And Layla? Ah, yes, Layla. A beautiful, angelic girl, a desirable girl. Perhaps, except for until you know the person well enough. The nurse girl. But as it was, only a trick, in the game of life, death, and love, between Michael and Jasmine Chivers.

'So that's how it is, Jasmine,' Michael said. 'Why can't I let you have the money? I mean---'

His voice stalled sapless, his eyes straying away from hers.

After a moment, Jasmine nodded. 'I know what you mean,' she said. 'I think I know.'

'Well,' he motioned, his hands suddenly awkward. 'It's certainly simple enough.'

'Yes,' Jasmine said. 'It's plain enough. Very plain. And it's something else, too.'

There was a strange glow in her eyes, an odd tightness to her face, a downcast harshness to her voice. Watching him, studying him, she slowly crossed one leg over the other.

'We're criminals, Michael. Let's face it.'

'We don't have to be, Jasmine. I'm turning over a new leaf. So can you.'

'But we've always had class. We've kept our private lives fairly straight. There were certain things we wouldn't do.'

'I know! So there's no difficulties! I can, we can'

The leg was swinging gently; hinting, speaking to him. Holding him hypnotized_.

'Michael, what if I told you I wasn't really your sister? That we are related first cousins?'

'Huh!' He looked down in Jasmine face shock. 'Why, I---'

'You'd like that, wouldn't you? Of course you would. You don't need to tell me. Now, why would you like it Michael?'

He swallowed disturbingly, attempted a laugh of assumed calmness. Everything was getting out of hand, out of his hands and into hers. The sudden awareness of his feelings, the sudden understanding of himself, all the terror and the joy and the desire held him thraldom and wordless.

'Michael. So softly that he could hardly hear it.

'Y-Yes?' He swallowed again. 'Yes?'

'I want that money, Michael. I've got to have it. Now, what do I have to do to get it?'

Jasmine, he said, or tried to say it, and perhaps he did say some of what he meant to. Jasmine, you know you can't go on like you were; you know you'll be caught, killed. You know I'm only trying to help you. If you didn't mean so much to me, I'd let you have the damned money. But I've got to stop you.'

'Maybe' she was going to be fair about this. 'You mean you really won't give it to me, Michael? You won't? Or will you? Can't I change your mind? What can I do to get it?'

And how could he tell her? How to say the unsayable?

Why don't you drink your water, dear? she said. And gratefully, welcoming this brief rest, Michael refused to drink the glass of water. And Jasmine, her grip stiff on the heavy hand bag, swung it with all her might.

Michael was quick, even for his tall size he ducked his head, swung his right leg and caught Jasmine ankles, tripping Jasmine to the floor. The handbag flew open, and the money spewed out in a green flood.

Jasmine looked at it bewilderedly. Michael wrapped one of his belts around her neck and squeezed her throat. He felt her pulse. It was over that swiftly.

He tied and wrapped her body in plastic. stowed her body on a shopping trolley, and took another look around the room.

All clear, it looked like. Her sister had been killed by Emily, by someone who didn't exist. Sure, Michael's own fingerprints and DNA were all over the room, but that wouldn't mean anything. The apartment holiday was Michael's home for four years.

Michael left the Park Royal and headed to Mr. Harper's friend's recycling yard. For the car to be crushed with Jasmine's lifeless body in the booth.

He wrote and sent the longest message of his life to Layla.

I wanted, as I have never wanted before, to take you on a nice vacation, to make you want to be mine, to carry you off and set you apart from all the strain and turmoil of the evil crimes recently happening in our city. For nothing will ever convince me that it is not the man's share in life to shield, to protect, to lead and toil and watch and battle with the world at large. I would like to be your knight in shining armor, my protector, my---I dare scarcely write the word--- my wife. So I am here beseeching. I am not yet twenty five, and I haven't been around the world as much as I'd like to be, and taste the quality of life.

Before I met you I never met anyone whom I felt I could love, but you have brought to light depths in my own nature I had scarcely suspected. Except for a few early burst of passion, natural to a warm and romantic disposition, and leaving no harmful after-effects--- outburst that by the standards of the higher truth I feel no one can justly cast a stone at, and of which I for one am by no means ashamed- --I come to you a pure and unchained young lad. I love you. I will try to offer you a life of wide and generous refinement, travel, and easy relations with a circle of brilliant and thoughtful people with whom my work has brought me into contact, and of which, seeing me only as you have done alone in this settlement, you can have no idea. that I am convinced you would not only furnish but delight in.

'I find it very hard to write these pages. There are so many things I want to tell you, and they stand on such different levels, that the effect is necessarily confusing and jarring, and I find myself doubting if I am really giving you the storyline of emotion that should run through all this Email. For although I must admit it reads very much like a petition or a testimonial or some such thing as that, I can assure you I am writing this in qualm and shaking with a sinking heart. My mind is full of motives and images that I have been cherishing and gathering up dreams of traveling side by side, of dining quietly together in some high spirits restaurant, of moonlight and music and all that side of life, of seeing you dressed like a queen or perhaps a radiant princess and shining in some brilliant mass; of your looking at flowers in some beautiful garden.

You know the saying, as, indeed, I have mentioned already, that most letters or notes are written in a state of emotion, but I have no doubt that this is true of lovely offers of long and lasting love. I have often felt before that it is only when one has nothing to say that one can write easy metrical composition. How can I get into one brief letter the complicated growing desires of what is now. My very knees stumbled and gave way. But I don't even care if I am ludicrous. I am a determined lad, and up until now when I have wanted a thing, I have got it; but I have never yet wanted anything in my life as I have wanted you. It isn't the same thing. I am afraid because I love you, so that the mere thought of failure hurts. If I did not love you so much, I believe I could win you by total duress of character, for quite often people tell me, I am naturally the controlling type. Most of my successes in life have been made with a sort of impulsive fine fettle.

Layla read the message through with deep, attentive eyes. Her interest grew as she read, a certain happiness appeared on her face. She smiled a few times. Then she went back to the kitchen and made herself another brew. Finally she fell into reflection.

The perception that they both were in love flooded Layla's mind and made changes to the standard of all its topics.

Michael began to think persistently of committing his future to Layla, and it seemed to him now that for some days at least he must have been thinking persistently of her unawares. He was surprised to find how stored his mind was with impressions and pleasant memories of Layla, how graphically he remembered her motions and little things that she had said. It occurred to Michael that it was silly to be so continuously thinking of one intriguing topic, and he made a spirited effort to force his mind to other questions.

But it was astounding that seemingly not to the point things could restore him to the thought of the enjoyable time they've spent together. And when he daydreams, then always gratifying feelings become the novel and wonderful guest of Michael's dreams.

For a time it really seemed all-sufficient to him that he should love. That Layla might love him seemed beyond the scope of his imagination. Indeed, he did not want to think of her as loving him. He wanted to think of her as his beloved future wife, to be near her and watch her, to have her going on nice holidays'. To think of him as loving her would make all that different. Then he would turn his face to her, and she would have to think of herself in his eyes. She would become caring, what she did would be the thing that mattered. He would want a long and lasting true love of her, and she would be passionately concerned to meet his requirements. Loving was better than that. Loving was self-forgetfulness, pure delighting in another human being. Michael felt that with Layla, whenever he was near to her, she would be content always to go on loving.

Chapter 27

A few weeks had flown by on the wings of love. Layla's and Michael's relationship was blooming. Michael started a new job in the Bahamas, working as a fire officer, he wanted to contribute to the upkeep of their new property. Layla got a nursing job at one of the hospitals. It is always delightful to wake up in a new bedroom. The fresh wallpaper, the strange but lovely pictures, the positions of doors and windows, imperfectly grasped the night before, are revealed with all the charm of surprise when they open their eyes each and every morning.

They stretched themselves deliciously in their great plumed four-post bed, and nursed each other's waking thoughts, and stared at the curious patterned awning above them. Layla and Michael were very pleased with the master bedroom, which certainly was chic and fascinating, and recalled the shapely interiors of the elegant rooms. Through the tiny parting of the long, flowered window curtains, they caught a peep of the sunlit lawns outside, the silver fountains, the bright flowers, and a gardener at work.

'Oh my,' he whispered, and turned round to freshen the frilled silk pillows behind him; 'and what delightful pictures,' he continued, wandering with his eyes from print to print that hung upon the rose-striped walls.

After Michael got up, he slipped off his dainty night wear, posturing elegantly before a long mirror, and made much of himself. Then with a white silk sash he draped himself in a few charming ways. So engrossed was he with his mirrored shape that he had not noticed the entrance of Layla, who stood admiringly but respectfully at a close distance, ready to receive her passionate morning kisses. As soon as Michael observed her he smiled sweetly, and squeezed Layla tightly in his arms, then he smiled sweetly, and prepared the bath.

The bathroom was the largest and perhaps the most beautiful apartment in his splendid suite. The well-known engraving by Lorette that forms the frontispiece will give you a better idea than any words of mine of the construction and decoration of the room. Only, in Lorette's engraving, the bath sunk into the middle of the floor is a little too small.

'Won't you join me?' Michael said, turning to layla who stood ready with warm towels and sweet body fragrances. In a moment they were free of their light morning dress, and jumped into the water and joined hands with a laughing link.

However, it is not so much at the very bath itself, as in the drying and delicious frictions, that a bather finds his chiefest pleasures, and Michael was more than satisfied with the skill his beloved Layla displayed. any thoughts of morning laziness he might have felt before was utterly dispelled. After he had rested a little, and sipped his hot chocolate drink, and ate some toast, they wandered around the beautiful garden.

'You're such a dear!' whispered Michael, holding Layla's hand.

'Our home is a tub of love,' said Layla softly.

The garden was an enchanted place where all the flowers seemed white, red,yellow, and pink. The lilies, the daphnes, the orange-blossom, the white stocks, the pink and red roses, you could see these as clearly as in the day-time; but the colored flowers existed only as a fragrance.

Now Michael was not the man to hurt anything if he could help it; besides, he was completely bewildered. Layla was clinging to him as she had not clung to anyone, and murmuring love, and welcoming him. It was a very joyous and fulfilling experience and she rested the softness of her cheek against his, and the lovely, sweet smell of her.

Michael could not help it; he put his arms around Layla, and kissed her; he was kissing her almost as tenderly as she was kissing him. In fact he could not stop kissing; and it was he now who began to speak in hushed tones, to say love things in her ear under her hair that smelt so nice and tickled him just as he remembered it used to tickle him. He held her close to his heart and her arms were soft round his neck.

Sunset gleams shone through the city. The joy of people finding an appreciative eye for all this beauty the city had to offer. Men gaze lingering longest upon the ladies at the afternoon lunch social gathering. The residents were happy, almost too happy, they sometimes thought, and therefore made most of their opportunities in their sweet cup of life.

How yellow the stars, and calm and true! How they blazed at their single task! And the wind moaned. Michael and Layla felt all the sadness, mystery, and nobility of this lonely haste, and full of their hearts rested the supreme consciousness that all would someday be well with the troubled world beyond.

The town was living again in one of its romances. so wild, merry, and full of joy. Love was no stranger to that lonely fleetness. The residents of the town were thrilled to their depth. The buildings stood tall and clear. Fireworks went shooting as if they were reaching for noble stars, not just the most beautiful. But the most elegant evening sky you will ever see. All that vast isolation breathed and waited, charged full with its secret, ready to reveal itself to her shaking soul.

Layla came into Michael's arms as he stared into her angel eyes. Michael's first kisses were on her lips, hard and cool and clean, like the life of a man. He kissed her again, and she hid her blushes in his passionate embrace. And it ended there beneath the sparkling eyes of their younger selves gazing on the beautiful city filled with beautiful lives.

Wayne Lawson

Wayne Lawson is a multi award winning writer. He has won two health and wellbeing book awards and three accolades for his work in the mental health field.

In his leisure time, he enjoys working out at the gym, singing at parties, and baking.

www.youtube.com/@waynelawson-q5j

www.ingramcontent.com/pod-product-compliance
Ingram Content Group UK Ltd.
Pitfield, Milton Keynes, MK11 3LW, UK
UKHW031825150325
456310UK00001B/41

9 781913 460877